HIGHLAND SECRETS

HIGHLAND FANTASY ROMANCE

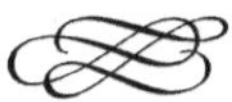

ANN GIMPEL

CONTENTS

COPYRIGHT PAGE

Publishing history: This book was released by Ann Gimpel and Dream Shadow Press as on 9/8/2015, and a brief excerpt is included in Wicked Alphas Wild Nights Set 1 that released on 9/27/15
ISBN Paperback: 978-1-948871-13-6
ISBN E-Book: 978-1-943849-05-5

BOOK DESCRIPTION: HIGHLAND SECRETS

Furious and weary, Angus Shea wants out, but he can't stop the magic powering his visions. The Celts kidnapped him when he wasn't much more than a boy. He's sick of them and their endless assignments, but they wiped his memories, and he has no idea where he came from.

Arianrhod prefers to work alone and guards her privacy for the best of reasons. She's not exactly a virgin, and she'd be laughed out of the Pantheon if the truth surfaced. Despite the complications of leading a double life, she's never found a lover who tempted her to walk away from the Celtic gods.

Dragon shifters are disappearing from the Scottish Highlands. The Celtic Council sends Angus and Arianrhod to Fire Mountain, the dragons' home world. Attraction ignites, so urgent Arianrhod's carefully balanced life teeters on the brink of discovery.

Can they risk everything?

Will they?

If they do, can they live with the consequences?

CHAPTER 1

*A*ngus Shea stroked beneath icy waters off the northern tip of Ireland, blending his energy with a pod of Selkies. The sea creatures cut through choppy waves in front, behind, and above him. He'd rather dive and play in the deeps with them—and if it were any other day, he would have—but he needed to keep an eye on the skies, so he edged toward the surface, pushing his head free.

Celene, a coal black Selkie he'd done more than swim with, drew close enough her lush pelt stroked his skin. He draped an arm around her, and she nuzzled his neck with her snout.

"Where have you been?" She spoke deep into his mind. Accommodating vocal chords were part of her human form, not her seal, and he'd never learned the Selkies' lyrical language.

"I spent a little time at my home in Scotland, but mostly I've ranged far from the Irish Sea."

"That doesn't tell me anything." She nipped playfully at his shoulder with her squared-off teeth.

"Prying ears are everywhere." He leaned into her warmth, enjoying a respite from the cold water.

"We could go where no one would hear."

He was tempted, so tempted he toyed with saying yes and

taking a break from watching for the dragon he expected. Dragons interpreted time in their own way, and the damned thing might not show up today or tomorrow or even this week. If it showed at all.

How much could he tell the Selkie?

An answer crowded on the heels of his question.

Nothing.

Angus shuttered his mind, so the creature swimming by his side couldn't read it. Much as he yearned to talk with someone, anyone, about the impossibilities the gods tasked him with, prudence won out. Not that this assignment was worse than any of the others, but he'd finally figured out they'd never end.

I could say no. Tell them I'm done.

He cut off the bitter laugh that wanted out. Whoever had the balls to refuse the Celts risked swift and certain punishment. He could hear Gwydion, master enchanter, or Ceridwen, goddess of the world, laughing their heads off—before they cut out his tongue or killed him on the spot.

"You don't have to say a word." Celene went on, almost as if she'd peeked into his thoughts before he took care to protect them. Selkie laughter buffeted him, spraying him with a warm, rich melody mixed with salty water. *"I'm curious, but I miss your body."*

He missed hers too. She'd been his only break from solitude for more years than he wanted to admit. He cast another glance skyward. Though he tried to be subtle, he heard a smug murmur near his ear and knew he hadn't fooled the Selkie.

"You wait for an Ancient One." The tenor of her mind speech shifted as she shielded it from anyone who might be close. Without stopping for him to corroborate, she forged ahead. *"We can take up the banner and watch for you. My kin will let us know."*

Angus picked his way carefully, as if he walked through a field of unexploded ordnance. "I appreciate the thought, but no one can know of my comings or goings, lass."

"We know more than you think." Celene batted him with a flipper.

"In truth, very little escapes us, but here isn't the place to share what I heard about your latest mission."

Concern rippled through him. If the Selkies knew, who else might? Hell, he didn't know much beyond his assigned meeting place with the dragon, and they'd be heading into danger.

What else was new? Danger was so second nature, his adrenaline pumps barely flinched at anything these days.

"Come with me." Either Celene was oblivious to the turmoil rumbling through him, or she ignored it. She swam from beneath his arm and herded him toward shore. *"There's a secluded glade deep in marsh grass. No one will find us, and my kin will keep watch for the dragon. I already asked."*

The Selkies would do their best—and maybe today it would be enough—but they were no match for evil that had sunk its roots deep into the fabric of the Old Country and the rest of this world. It was why the gods stooped to using him—half-mortal, half-divine, or whatever the hell he was—to do their dirty work. Arawn, god of the dead, revenge, and terror, caught him skulking in the time-travel tunnels when he wasn't much more than a boy and trapped him, cutting off any possibility of return. To make certain Angus remained, the god altered his memories, so he had no idea where he came from.

Now almost twenty-five years later, Arawn and the others still came up with enough for him to do that a life to call his own was out of the question. The carrot they dangled was the truth about his birth, but they never came close to divulging it. The stick was his fear of what they'd do, if he told them he was done.

Over time, he'd stopped asking about his origins. He cared, but it wasn't worth the energy to run up against their stony faces and cunningly crafted half-truths that revealed exactly nothing. Despite his reservations about a quick dalliance with Celene—and maybe missing his rendezvous with the dragon—he was sick of his self-imposed isolation.

She chivied him into shallow water. Once she was certain he'd follow, she drew ahead easily. As if the other Selkies understood, the pod dispersed. When he peered through gray-green water for their multi-colored pelts, they weren't there.

By the time he clambered onto the rocky shore, Celene had shucked her skin. In human form, she opened her arms to welcome him. Long black hair shrouded her almost to her feet. Violet eyes gleamed in welcome. Her generous breasts peeked through the curtain of hair, their copper-colored nipples already pebbled with wanting him.

Angus had tucked his clothes beneath a rock before joining the Selkie pod. Because he swam nude, nothing was in the way as he plunged into Celene's offered embrace. God, how he'd missed the touch of another against him, skin to skin. Celene's body felt warm against his chilled one. She closed her arms around him and ran her hands down his back, lingering over the curve of his butt.

He hugged her in return. The scent of her, salt and mint, flooded his mind with images of their lovemaking, and his cock hardened between their bodies. He trailed his fingertips down her smooth skin, marveling at how different she felt from a human woman. Velvety and charged with electricity. Some Selkies walked among humans, even took permanent partners. Angus didn't understand how they eluded discovery.

Celene closed her mouth over the junction between his neck and shoulder, licking, sucking, biting. He moved a hand from her back to cup the side of her face and lowered his lips over hers. Desire engulfed him. Hot, urgent, desperate, he sank his tongue into her waiting mouth.

She grappled with his ass, pulling his body hard against hers as her hips writhed and breath hitched in her throat. Tearing her mouth from his, she gasped. "Too long. It's been too long."

Liquid heat trailed the path of her mouth as she licked her way down his chest, stopping to tease his nipples. He kissed the top of her head and wove his fingers into her long hair. Every nerve came alive with wanting her, but it ran deeper than that. Touch was such a basic need, and he'd denied that essential part of his humanity—along with every other comfort.

For what?

No matter how much he gave the Celts, they took every shred—and him—for granted. He wanted to get a job, blend in with humans. Something mundane like driving a cab, or flipping burgers in a grill, but his requests were denied. The Celts provided for him. So long as they housed and fed him, why would he need to clutter his time with anything as humdrum as earning a living? What if they needed him, and he was in the middle of washing dishes in some nameless restaurant? He could almost hear Gwydion's voice. See the master enchanter with a long-suffering look on his face—

He wiped his Celtic masters from his mind. This time was for him and Celene. No one else belonged in his head. Just because he'd chosen a semimonastic existence was no reason he couldn't give her everything she needed. Months had passed since they'd last been together, maybe as much as a year. He moved back enough to fill his hands with her breasts, rubbing her erect nipples before he bent to suck on them, remembering the little biting motions she loved.

A low, guttural moan escaped her, and she threaded her fingers through his hair. Holding him against her breasts, she began to sing as he loved her. A series of low, sweet notes rose in cadence and intensity as she lost herself in his touch. He'd asked her about the music once, and she told him it was how sea people vocalized their joy. The music filled him with unbearable hunger—poignant, mind-bending need for another person's touch.

Although he'd never done it before, he raised his voice and joined her song. The change was instantaneous. In that moment, he sensed her loneliness and isolation, twin to his own and recognized that both of them needed more kisses, more touches—even more than they needed sex.

"Lay on your belly." His voice rasped with wanting her. He tore tufts of marsh grass and arranged them to make her a bed on a sandy stretch between rocks.

She lay down, continuing to sing. Angus sang too, as he straddled her and ran his hands down her back rubbing tension from her muscles. He followed his hands with his mouth and strung kisses across her shoulder blades and down the line of vertebrae from her neck to the curves of her ass. Between their song, the feel of her skin beneath his fingertips, and his cock getting stiffer by the moment, waiting became almost painful, yet he held back, not quite sure why.

The rhythm and cadence of her song shifted as he alternated his mouth and hands across the sculpted planes of her back. The intense pressure in his balls receded almost as if he'd reached a peak, though he hadn't come. Maybe she sensed his need for warmth, contact, much as he'd sensed hers.

"Move off me so I can look at you." Celene flipped over to face him, kneeling above her. Rose and gold splotched her pale skin, and a broad smile split her exotic, high-cheek-boned face. "Today was different. You sang with me. You've never done that before."

He shrugged, suddenly self-conscious. "It felt right. Even though I wasn't inside you, what happened between us felt right."

She cocked her head to one side and trained her gaze on him. "Are you sure you don't have sea blood?"

A flicker of annoyance at the Celts' staunch refusal to disclose anything about his birth narrowed his eyes. "I have no idea what I am." He ticked what he did know off on his fingers. "I'm not immortal, but I'll live well beyond human lifespans. My magic is closer to seer and witch than anything else, yet I'm neither of those. The covens acknowledge me as one of theirs, but only because the local witches are too kind to tell me to go away. The time-travel portals accept me." He shrugged again. "I don't suppose knowing more would make a hell of a lot of difference."

"You're not from Scotland, even though you live there." She stated it baldly, as fact.

He frowned. "Why would you say that?"

"Your speech. There's something about the lilt of Scotland that's impossible to rid yourself of. You don't sound Irish or British, either, at least not from the time we live in." Her nostrils flared. "Maybe that's it."

"Maybe what's it?"

"You could be from the past, and not just a few years back, perhaps hundreds—or even more. I'm not old enough to recall what human speech sounded like then, but some Selkies are."

"Fine." Frustration tightened his chest, like it always did when the mystery of his origins became a point of discussion. "My first memories are when the god of the dead dragged me out of a time-travel portal when I was fifteen."

"I'm sorry." She draped a hand over his hip, cradling it. "I've upset you."

He started to protest, but she silenced him with a look. "Don't insult me with a lie, Angus, but you don't have to talk about it, either. Such a pretty man." She stroked hair back from his face. "With your deep brown hair and amber eyes. Did you know they shade to dark gold when you're angry?"

She was trying to divert him with flattery, but he wasn't buying it. "You have no idea what it's like not knowing—" He shook his head, and the rest of his words died unspoken. It didn't matter what she knew or didn't know about him. She'd never be more than an occasional lover, and both of them knew it.

"It could be more," she said softly, obviously having been in his mind.

Angus took her hands in his and gazed at her. "You get more of me than anyone, and you see how pathetically little that is. There's nothing more to give."

"There could be," she persisted. "You could refuse next time they send you on—"

He bent toward her and laid a hand over her mouth. "I'm not free. Not now. Not ever."

"I don't understand." She pushed his hand away and closed very white teeth over her full lower lip.

He smiled crookedly. "Not sure I do, either. Every man has a life's work. No matter how I feel about it, this appears to be mine."

Even though it wasn't wise, he started to ask what she knew about his current assignment, but a flash of unusual energy drew his gaze skyward. He leapt to his feet. A copper-colored dragon circled to land not far from him. Maybe the Ancient One had seen him with Celene and decided to be considerate.

Not very fucking likely. Dragons were a force unto themselves.

"I have to go," he said. "Let me walk you to your skin, so I know you're safely on your way home."

A sad expression crossed her face, creasing the skin around her eyes into a network of fine lines. "It's right here." She scrambled to her feet and gripped both his upper arms, forcing him to look at her. "Thank you."

"For what?"

"Being you." She brushed her lips over his and moved to a marsh grass thicket. In moments, she'd dragged her pelt over her human body. Transformed into a seal, she waded into the surf.

Before it engulfed her, she turned to gaze at him. *"Be careful, and think on what I said."*

He didn't answer, just watched her head bob in the waves before turning toward his clothing. It wasn't far from the place Celene had led them. His body felt vibrant, alive, and he still tingled from her touch. He longed for a woman of his own, children, a home, before he stuffed the impossible so deep under wraps he couldn't mourn the loss.

Angus moved the large rock he'd placed over his clothes to protect them from the wind. He pulled a ragged dark blue fisherman's knit sweater over his head and stepped into thick, black woolen trousers. Settling on a log, he pulled on socks and laced up stout leather boots. Though the breeze was raw, he'd worn neither hat nor gloves.

Ready as he figured he'd ever be, he covered the fifty yards to where the dragon had settled up the beach. He didn't recognize this one, but he'd only met a bare handful of the hundreds living in Fire Mountain and on other worlds as well. When he drew near, he stopped and bowed his head respectfully, waiting for the dragon to speak first.

"I don't like this any better than you do," the dragon muttered. "Come close enough I don't have to broadcast our business to the world."

Angus walked closer. He could've suggested the dragon use telepathy since all the Ancient Ones were conversant in the technique, but he kept his mouth shut. The dragon was smaller than many he'd seen. Copper scales shaded to burnished gold on its chest, and dark eyes with golden centers whirled so fast they held a hypnotic quality. Lethal, six-inch-long red claws tipped its stubby forelegs. The dragon stood upright on hind legs tipped with the same sharp claws and kept its gaze averted, not saying anything.

What the hell? Every other dragon he'd met was proud, imperious, and quick to remind Angus of his inferiority. This one seemed young, but was it? After another long few minutes, Angus tossed respect—and caution—to the winds.

"What's your name? And what are we supposed to be doing? All Ceridwen told me was to meet you here."

The dragon opened its mouth, and a gout of flame landed scant inches from Angus's boots.

He frowned and drew his brows together. "If we're going to work together, I need to know what to call you." He sent a speculative gaze across the air between them. "If you annihilate me, they'll just assign you a new partner, and I'm a hell of a lot easier to get along with than any of the Celts."

"Tell me something I don't know," the dragon rumbled and belched smoke.

Frustration in its voice struck a note in Angus's soul, and he gestured with both hands. "You may as well tell me who you are and what we're supposed to do together." He infused his words with subtle persuasion. If the dragon didn't care for the Celts, either, they'd likely get along well enough.

"Why? What I should do is leave." The dragon sounded sulky—and scared.

"If you could, you'd already be gone." Angus was as certain of that as he was of anything. The dragon needed him for something, and whatever it was, the Ancient One wasn't particularly proud of it. "What happened? Am I some sort of punishment for you?" Tension settled like a steel bar across his shoulders, and he curled his hands into fists before he realized what he'd done.

"Oh I'd be gone, would I?"

The dragon ignored Angus's questions, and it mimicked his tone with eerie precision. It furled its wings and flapped them a time or two. Dirt swirled; small pebbles slapped Angus in the face. The creature belched steam and looked so distraught, he felt sorry for it.

"My life's not exactly a picnic, either," he ventured, on a hunt for common ground. "I'm a permanent mercenary, with no time off and no possibility of parole."

That got the dragon's attention, and it focused its whirling gaze on him. The golden centers of its eyes deepened with fiery motes that looked like little shooting stars. "Why would you want a respite from being a warrior?"

Good question.

"Because I'm tired. I'd like what most men have."

"What's that?" The dragon raised its brows, and its scales clanked against each other in a dissonant tinkling.

He shook his head. "It doesn't matter. The sooner you spit out whatever you need to say, the easier it'll be. The worst part about holding something you're ashamed of inside is it eats at you until you're nothing but a hollow shell."

Wings flapped, and those intense, whirling eyes shifted to the rocky beach. "I'm not *ashamed* of anything. I've been banished. Ceridwen said if I worked with you—and we were successful—I might be able to return."

Angus kept surprise out of his voice. "Banished from Fire Mountain?"

Steam puffed from the dragon's open mouth. "No. Idiot. I could live with that. They've banished me from the Highlands. My home."

"What happened?"

"It doesn't matter." The dragon threw his words back at him. "We have to go to Fire Mountain, where I'm to find one of the First Born. Once we have him—or her—"

"One of the six First Born dragons?" Angus broke in, scarcely believing the dragon's words. "They'll never show themselves— unless it's in their best interest."

Another wing flap and a defiant head toss. "There are actually ten. One of them was my father."

"When's the last time you saw him?" The words slipped out before he could stop them. Dragon males frequently didn't hang about once mating was over with, but the trembling mass of scales in front of him likely didn't need to be reminded.

"Never. Mother said he was too immersed in battles on another world to return for our hatching."

Angus unclenched his fists and hunted for something soothing to say that wasn't an outright lie. Dragon energy poked past his wards and into his mind. He tried to block it, but couldn't.

"You believe locating a First Born is hopeless." The dragon sounded resigned. "I may as well throw myself into a crater at Fire Mountain. I'll never see the Highlands again—or my mate." More wing rustling and the dragon rose a few feet off the ground, clearly intent on leaving.

"Hold on." Angus loped forward until he was right beneath the dragon. "I didn't say that—or think it, either. I don't know enough to make any sort of judgment. How about if you start at the beginning? If we're going to work together, I deserve that much."

The dragon circled a few times, indecision stamped in its erratic flight pattern.

"I know what it is to be alone." He kept his voice gentle. "And to not have anyone who cares if I live or die."

Maybe it wasn't totally true. Celene might shed a tear or two, but she'd be the only one. He kept his gaze trained on the sky, relieved the dragon wasn't putting distance between them. Something about the creature's pain tugged at his heart and made it feel like a kindred spirit.

The copper dragon folded its wings and settled heavily to earth a few feet from where Angus stood. It straightened its shoulders and tipped its chin defiantly.

"My name is Eletea," the dragon announced, revealing its gender.

"Angus Shea, though you likely know that."

"Yes, I do. I killed a mage, who fancied herself a dragon shifter." Eletea's eyes whirled faster, as if she dared Angus to say something.

He crinkled his forehead as he dredged up what he knew about dragon shifters. "Don't mages take their chances when they show up seeking a dragon to pair with?"

She nodded once, sharply. "The mage seduced one of us into believing her. I saved him by killing her, but he turned on me. Reported me to the Dragons' Council, and they roped the Celts into deciding my fate, since the one I killed had Celtic blood." Eletea's scales rippled in the dragon equivalent of a shrug. "I don't understand why they're bothering. It's not like I went after one of the gods. They're immortal. The one all the fuss is over barely qualified as a Celt."

Angus kept his expression neutral. "Celtic blood aside, I thought mages only bonded with same sex dragons."

"That was another problem," Eletea said, sounding vindicated. "No one saw it but me, though."

Sensing the worst was out on the table, Angus settled on a nearby rock and invited, "Start at the beginning. We have time."

"No, we don't," Eletea protested. "We should've been at Fire Mountain yesterday." She hung her head. "I didn't know what I wanted to do, so I flew and flew and flew. I almost didn't land this afternoon."

Angus did his best to project optimism. "Let's open a time-travel portal and be on our way to Fire Mountain." At the dragon's reluctant nod, he went on. "I understand you have your own ways of returning home, but if you travel with me, you can fill me in as we go."

What he didn't say was it probably wouldn't matter when they arrived at the dragons' home world. First Borns wouldn't give them the time of day, whether they showed up early, late, or right on time. He held many concerns, such as what would a First Born do, assuming they could locate one? But he held those cares inside for now.

He could've dreamed the future. Instead, he summoned a spell to take them to a time-traveling portal. Once the undulating gray-pink tube admitted them, he gradually paid out questions.

Reticent and quiet at first, Eletea finally began to talk.

CHAPTER 2

Arianrhod slumped lower in her chair, wishing she could find a graceful way to leave. The Celtic gods' council hall had been in Inverlochy Castle in the Scottish Highlands for centuries. To human eyes, the place lay in ruins, but magic could resurrect most anything. The afternoon's discussion had dragged on for hours, and she wanted nothing more than to slip out a side door and go hunting.

Or pour herself a stiff drink.

Or send a bolt of magic to silence the Morrigan permanently—if that were even possible.

She scanned the opulent room and tried to find something to focus on aside from the Battle Crow's ongoing rant. Twelve-foot-high oaken doors carved with runic symbols decorated one end of the room. Crystals and natural stone in every hue of the rainbow made a prism of sunlight flaring through leaded glass panes. Rich carpets covered the stone floors, thick wool woven with depictions of Celtic glory. A fire burned in an enormous hearth situated across from the entry doors.

Ceridwen sat in her usual place before the blaze, cauldron before her. From time to time, she stirred the bubbling mix with an enormous wooden staff. When she cleared her throat in a muttery growl, a handful of Celts looked up from where they'd scattered themselves about the room, no one too close to anyone else. If Arianrhod read their expressions correctly, they were as sick of the Morrigan's pontificating as she was.

Arianrhod straightened in her chair and came to her feet. Before she could open her mouth, the Battle Crow morphed into one of her other guises. Instead of a huge avian presence, she looked like a medieval noblewoman with long dark hair coaxed into intricate braids. Dark eyes regarded Arianrhod, and the Morrigan bent so her breasts almost spilled from her tightly cut maroon gown with long, daggéd sleeves.

With an eye roll, Arianrhod snapped, "Save it for the men. I've heard more than enough about your fourteenth cousin five times removed, who was killed by the young dragon. And about the dragon your kinswoman planned to bond with, demanding the other dragon's life. How many times can ye tell that tale, anyway? And why is this cousin so bleeding important?"

"Do ye want dragon shifters to die out entirely?" the Morrigan demanded.

Arianrhod shrugged. "Not certain I've given it much thought, but I canna see where it would make much difference. Magic wielders come and go."

"How can ye say such a thing?" the Morrigan screeched.

Ceridwen vaulted to her better than six-foot height. Long black hair streaked with silver fell to her knees, and her dark eyes mirrored an ever-changing collage of images. Body-hugging tan leather breeches and a hip-length tunic woven with green and golden thread covered her lithe frame. Knee-high leather boots wound up both legs. She extended an arm, index finger pointed at the Morrigan's chest.

"I, too, weary of this. Ye havena said aught new in the past turn of the glass. I declare this topic closed." She crossed her arms beneath her breasts and eyed the Morrigan, apparently expecting an argument. When she didn't get one, Ceridwen added, "I've taken care of the problem."

The Morrigan narrowed her dark eyes. "Really? How?"

"I sent the dragon in question, a young female named Eletea, to Fire Mountain to seek a First Born. They can read her intent and proclaim her guilty or innocent of malicious intent."

"Pfft." The Morrigan waved a dismissive hand. "How do ye know this Eletea will do your bidding?"

"Because I forbade her from returning to the Highlands, and I'm sending Angus with her." An arrogant smile crossed Ceridwen's ageless face. "Even if they doona find a First Born—and they may not—he can dream the truth."

A flicker of something between annoyance and fear crossed the Morrigan's features, turning them grim and threatening. Before Arianrhod could drill into what that expression meant, the Battle Crow morphed back into her avian form. Shrieking her displeasure, she flew out an open window.

"Would that it were always so easy to rid ourselves of that one," Andraste muttered. The goddess of victory, dressed in her usual tan battle leathers, rose to her feet, stretched her arms over her head, and glanced at the assemblage. "I'm leaving, if 'tis all the same to you." She tossed heavy blonde hair over her shoulders and swept her shrewd green eyes about the room in a clear challenge—should anyone question her right to go.

"Wait." Arianrhod faced the other woman. "We havena addressed the rumors of dragon shifters running amok along with their dragons. In truth, I doona think of it often, but the Morrigan's words—"

"Eletea will take that up with the dragons in Fire Mountain. 'Tis at the core of her rationale for murdering the dark mage," Ceridwen cut in and shifted her unsettling gaze to Arianrhod. "Since ye expressed interest, mayhap ye could meet them there."

"Them?" Arianrhod quirked a brow.

"Angus and the dragon." Ceridwen eyed her coolly. "Ye werena paying attention. I just said that."

"Sorry." Arianrhod didn't want to get into an argument. Easier to apologize and have done with it. "I'll go. No problem."

"Come closer."

Arianrhod walked until she stood nose to nose with Ceridwen, staring at the images marching across her eyes. What she saw made her heart beat faster. Blood ran in rivers around dying dragons, with a huge crow feasting on one of them. The goddess of the world was warning her to watch out for the Morrigan. And to take the renegade dragon shifter problem seriously.

Arianrhod opened her mouth, but Ceridwen shook her head and switched from imagery to deeply shielded mind speech. *"Lachlan and his dragon havena been seen for hundreds of years. They vanished without a trace. Britta and her dragon retreated to an earlier time. We must know if foul energy has infiltrated the dragon shifter bond. If incentives to tempt even the staunchest mage to dark power exist, I would know of them."*

A smile split Arianrhod's face, and she showed Ceridwen a mouthful of teeth. This was better than hunting game. Evil was the finest challenge of all. She inclined her head. "I welcome the assignment."

Ceridwen tossed her head back and laughed. "I dinna doubt ye would, not for a moment."

"Would ye care for company, sister?"

Gwydion, master enchanter and warrior magician, strode to where the women stood. He'd obviously been listening in on her private conversation with Ceridwen—or trying his damnedest to— which annoyed the hell out of Arianrhod. His long blond hair was done up in the Celtic warrior pattern of multiple small braids layered over each other, and his blue gaze augured into Arianrhod, no doubt seeking why she'd volunteered so readily. Gwydion favored robes. Today he wore black silk, sashed in red. The staff that never left his hand shone with a pale, white light. Its inner glow illuminated eldritch carvings running along its length in bas-relief.

Arianrhod wrenched her gaze away from the staff. It was as hypnotic as a cobra; she'd been trapped more than once trying to make out the runes streaked up and down its polished sides. She turned to face her brother squarely. "I can be far more unobtrusive if 'tis just me."

He drew his brows together into a thick, disapproving line. "Aye, but two can accomplish twice what one can." He waved his staff at Ceridwen. "Tell her she must allow me to accompany her."

"I'll do no such thing," the goddess of the world replied. "If she wishes your company, 'tis for her to request it."

"I'll call for you if I have need of reinforcements." Arianrhod forced a much cheerier smile than she felt and made her eyes guileless. Gwydion only offered to come along because he was bored. He didn't care a twit about helping her. Never had. They'd been at each other's throats since they were children.

Gwydion took a step back and mock bowed. "See ye do that… sister." With a sweep of his robe, he vanished.

"Good call." Ceridwen spoke into her ear. "The less anyone knows about why ye've decided to pay a visit to Fire Mountain, the better. Had two of us shown up, we'd need a stated reason. One the dragons would believe."

"That's the kicker, eh?" Arianrhod whispered back. "Not the most trusting race, dragons."

"Understatement, my dear. Now get moving and take care that brother of yours doesna follow your tracks."

"What about Angus? Ye sent him to Fire Mountain. Won't the dragons become suspicious?"

Ceridwen shot a wry smile skittering her way. "Och, the dragons adore seers, plus he isna one of the gods."

Arianrhod frowned. "Aye, I've never met him afore. What exactly is he?"

"Does it matter?" Ceridwen countered her question with

another, which meant she didn't plan to answer it. "He's helpful, which is all ye need to know."

Arianrhod cloaked herself in magic and summoned a traveling spell, aiming for her castle in the Scottish Highlands. She'd swathed the medieval structure in so many layers of invisibility, no one would ever be able to catch her by surprise. She was fairly certain Gwydion had no idea where she lived, and she aimed to keep it that way. Whitewashed stone walls formed around her, and she blew out a tightly held breath. Before she relaxed entirely, she sent power spinning in a wide arc to make certain she was alone.

Good.

No one had breached her home's defenses since she left. She stared around the great room, appreciating its simplicity. She'd never gone for the opulent wall hangings or rich carpets the other Celts preferred. Her home boasted broad, gray flagstone floors with the occasional throw rug to give chilled toes a break. Fireplaces graced every room, and she used them for heat, rather than installing more modern central heating. In truth, she preferred the crackle of wood to the *whoosh* of a forced air fan. Her manor house could've housed a hundred. There were rooms she hadn't laid eyes on in centuries. Mostly, she shuttled between the great room, the kitchens, her bedroom, and the room where she kept her bows and knifes. Guns had come into fashion, but she didn't care for them. Too noisy and bulky for her taste.

One concession to modern life was a green-veined marble bathroom off her bedroom with a hot-water-on-demand system. Nothing quite like drawing a bath without having to heat the water with magic. Another place she'd caved was installing a large, clunky computer, complete with access to a fledgling Internet. She didn't totally understand the Advanced Research Projects Agency NETwork, but it was useful for research—far easier than digging through tomes and scrolls in her enormous library.

Despite nagging from her Celtic kin, she'd drawn the line at a mobile phone—or any phone, for that fact. She could tap anyone she wanted telepathically, so she didn't need an electronic sidekick.

Whistling a wordless Gaelic folk song, she trotted into the armaments room and slid golden arrows into a quiver that she tossed over her shoulder. Next came a knife she tucked inside a thigh sheath. She picked a powerful crossbow, decided she didn't need anything further, and chanted to open a time-traveling portal. For years she'd transported herself to one of the entry points that would move her where she instructed. During a trip back from a depressing future where mankind had mostly annihilated Earth's resources, she'd accidentally ended up in the sub-basement of her castle.

That was how she knew her dwelling housed an entrance, and she'd used it shamelessly ever since. Why squander power if she didn't have to? A pearlescent, tubular structure formed before her. She walked through a portal and settled herself inside. Its walls were grayish and warm as if the conduit were alive. She chanted a different incantation to seal herself into the time shaft. Her magic held a pungent scent for this particular casting, like motor oil mixed with salt water.

Fire Mountain existed beyond time on a borderworld that shared a frequency with Earth. If it didn't, she suspected no one but dragons would be able to access it. The shaft vibrated as Arianrhod moved backward in time to the ancient dragon stronghold. She hunkered into a squat for the long journey, taking care not to touch the pulsing walls. No point in being jettisoned because she pissed off whatever—or whomever—infused life into the channel. That had happened more than once, and it took variable amounts of time before the guardian allowed her access again. Being stuck with dinosaurs—which had happened before—wasn't high on her list.

Excitement thrummed through her, and she considered how to proceed once she arrived at Fire Mountain. Mayhap she could pretend she was interested in pairing with a dragon. She narrowed her eyes and chewed thoughtfully on her lower lip. Should she join with Angus and the dragon, Eletea? Or pretend she knew nothing about them? If she chose to masquerade as a wannabe dragon shifter, would the Ancient Ones believe her?

"Why would they?" she muttered. "I haven't shown the slightest interest in anything dragon-related since the dawn of time." Perhaps she could tell them she was bored, that her life lacked meaning, purpose. All true. Immortality held a big downside, particularly since somewhere along the line, she'd fashioned herself as the virgin huntress.

Arianrhod rolled her mental eyes. Why the hell had she thought that was a good idea when Danu suggested it? At the time, she'd hoped to escape Bran's attentions, but she hadn't planned on millennia tossing and turning in an empty bed. The god of prophecy —Bran—was as big a pain in the ass as he'd always been, but at least he had a cock...

She winced. It had taken stealth and cunning to maintain her artfully crafted persona and still have a sex life. Nothing frequent enough to draw attention, but she'd lain with the occasional man— and an amazing coal black dragon. He'd worried his kin would shun him if their affair were discovered, but it hadn't made a dent in his hunger for her.

Nothing quite like the forbidden to fan those flames...

Truth smacked her between the eyes. Loneliness and lust were why she'd volunteered so readily to make the trek to Fire Mountain. And why she'd sidestepped Gwydion. The last thing she needed was a witness if she stumbled onto Keene—or another likely candidate. Dragons lived practically forever. Perhaps Keene might be interested in another fling—for old time's sake if nothing else.

Usually she stopped herself from thinking about her past and what she wished she'd done differently, but she couldn't shut off her thoughts. If she'd had children, real children, it would've made such a difference.

The two sons she'd conceived magically were odd. But how could they have been aught else? She'd been forced to jump over a magical rod to prove she was a virgin, and twin sons were the result. Dylan sank into obscurity, retreating to the seas when the strain of day-to-day life without enough power to light a candle became too much to bear. Lleu would've left as well, but Gwydion subverted every single one of Lleu's escape plans as he grew to manhood. Lleu blamed her for Gwydion's meddling, and she hadn't laid eyes on him for a very long time. She suspected Gwydion hadn't, either.

Her empty life mocked her, but she was damned if she could figure out what to do to change it. It wasn't as if she could march up to Ceridwen and the others, clear her throat, and say, "Sorry, but I'm sick of being a Celtic god. Think I'll be a mortal for a while. And hey, if that doesn't please you, I'll take to my owl form and be done with the lot of you.

"Oberon's balls!" She crashed one fist into an open hand, taking care not to jostle the traveling portal. "I have to pull my head out of my ass. Ceridwen handed me a fascinating problem. I need to focus on it. No dragon fucking. No diversions. Go in. Put my head down. Get the job done."

Nice lecture, but can I do it?

Arianrhod stroked the shiny bow draped over her shoulder. It was a work of art. She'd made it herself from yew wood, not cutting any corners, so it took months for the wood to shape and cure. She twisted her mouth into a wry smile. The huntress part of her title was fine. It fit, and she enjoyed the cunning, planning, and forethought it took to outsmart prey. If she was sick of the pretend-to-be-a-virgin part, who could blame her?

The rhythm of her traveling tube shifted. Arianrhod glanced at a node to check her location and understood her journey would be over soon. She rotated her shoulders to relax and ready herself, thought about her virgin huntress title once more, and laughed.

"The virgin part may grate, but I adore being a huntress. Fifty percent isn't bad," she told the gray-pink walls as they shuddered to a stop. "Most people don't even get that."

CHAPTER 3

"The mage you killed courted the dragon for seven years?" Angus asked Eletea, not quite understanding why it would take so long for a dragon to make up its mind about… Well, about anything.

"Might've been closer to eight, but she wasn't there all the time." The dragon repositioned herself.

It was cramped in the time-travel shaft, worse for Eletea than for him, since she was so much larger. The tunnel stretched to accommodate its occupants, but it didn't leave any extra room.

"Say more about that." Angus made a come-along gesture with one hand.

"Good thing my dragon friend and the mage weren't in any rush, or I'd never have been able to discern anything was amiss." She furrowed her scaled brow in thought. "Not that dragon shifters are a common occurrence, but enough candidates showed up, none of us paid them much heed. Unless they wanted to bond with us."

"Were you ever chosen?" Angus asked, curious.

She shook her head to the accompaniment of jangling scales, bathing him with steam and soft dragon laughter. "Targeted might be a better word than chosen." She laughed again. "For one thing,

I'm too young. For another, I joined my life to a Highland dragon's, which meant I left Fire Mountain."

Angus poked around for a delicate way to phrase his next question, gave up, and asked, "Where'd you kill the mage?"

"Why is that important?" Eletea countered, regarding him with her whirling eyes.

"Likely it's not, but if I summon a vision to see the event clearly, the more facts I have, the more accurate my revelations are."

"I don't get it." Smoke puffed past her double rows of teeth. "What's there to see in a sending? I told you all of it."

"Nay. You told me your side of things. Visions hold all aspects. Besides…" He hurried on. "You've scarcely shared *all of it*."

"I told you the parts I deemed important."

Angus narrowed his eyes and checked a node as it flashed past. They'd have at least another half hour, perhaps more, before the tunnel spit them out. He inhaled deeply, before pushing the breath out and doing it again. "How about if you tell me all of it, and let me judge what's important."

The dragon was silent for long moments. When she began to talk again, her words were halting, as if she wasn't certain what she wanted to say.

"Danne—the dragon I was trying to save—and the woman who wanted to bond with him showed up in the Highlands to visit me and my mate. I hadn't seen either of them in the years since I left Fire Mountain with Cavet to make our home on the Isle of Skye."

"What was the purpose of their visit?"

"Danne and I were close—"

"How close?" Angus demanded. "Was he your intended before Cavet?"

She spread her jaws in a smile. "Nothing like that. He and I were egg-mates."

Angus sensed there had to be more to it. "You must've had many egg-mates. What was special about him?"

"There were fifteen in my clutch," she concurred, "but Danne and I came from the same egg."

"Is that even possible?" Angus narrowed his eyes as he considered it.

"Of course it's possible." She bristled. "I'm here, aren't I? But it is quite rare, and Danne and I share a bond I never felt with the other dragons in our clutch."

Curiosity stirred in Angus, and he leaned forward. "What happened during their visit?"

"I've asked myself the same thing. Darkness shrouded the woman. Mitha was her name, and the same darkness clouded Danne's mind. It was much worse than when I'd last seen him. So bad, he scarcely had any capacity left for independent thought. I drew him off, just the two of us, on the pretext of hunting, and tried to talk with him. He and Mitha were not yet bonded, so I held hope he'd see reason."

"Never works that way," Angus cut in, and then kicked himself for not holding his tongue. "Go on." He made shooing motions with one hand. "Sorry for interrupting."

Eletea nodded slowly. "Once the bond is forged, it's quite difficult to sunder, yet Danne refused my counsel. He acted as if he and Mitha were already joined. After we returned, I conferred with Cavet in our private mind speech. I was afraid Mitha knew I didn't trust her, and I wanted time to develop a course of action. Cavet advised staying out of it, but I couldn't stand by and let that dark witch co-opt my friend to evil."

She lowered her voice, almost as if she suspected the time-travel shaft held prying ears. "Some dragons bonded to shifters have disappeared. Others, like Malik and Preki, boast of powers few dragons possess. Their bonded mages hold the same dark energy as Mitha." Eletea's face developed a pinched look. "I know I'm young and untried, but I couldn't stand by and allow Danne to consecrate his bond to Mitha. I couldn't. If it had been any other dragon, I'd probably have stepped aside, but not Danne. Not my egg-mate."

"How'd you do it?" Angus asked, impressed by her courage and determination. "Powerful mages are hard to kill."

Eletea's eyes whirled faster. "Only hard after she and Danne bonded, which was another reason I had to move quickly. If I'd waited, she'd have become immortal along with her dragon. I flattered her, took her flying, and made certain she didn't come back."

The dragon swallowed hard, the motion moving down her sinuous neck. "When I returned, I told Danne and Cavet what I'd done. Danne challenged me to a duel to the death in direct combat." She swallowed again. "I was shocked, my spirit wounded, yet I fought. Mostly to protect myself. I couldn't bring myself to hurt Danne." Eletea shook her head sadly. "If Cavet hadn't intervened, Danne might've killed me."

She belched fire this time, not steam, her dark eyes defiant. Flames bounced off the walls of the time-travel shaft, and the chamber shuddered around them. "Sorry." Eletea patted a gray-pink wall. "No more fire."

She refocused on Angus and clanked her jaws in frustration. "Danne left, knowing he couldn't fight us both. It gets even better, though—or worse, depending how you look at things. Danne hadn't even cleared our skies before Cavet gave me a good dressing down. He was still chastising me when Ceridwen showed up."

"Bad news travels fast."

"You could say that." Eletea tossed her head. "You know the rest. A First Born can either vindicate me or condemn me." She hesitated. "Cavet's waiting for the verdict too."

Angus bit back words. He wanted to tell her that a mate who didn't believe in her was far worse than no mate at all, but what did he know of such things? Instead he said, "I can dream the truth of this too. At least now I understand why Ceridwen sent you to me."

"Excellent." She clasped her taloned forelegs together. "Then we shall see an end to this soon, and I can return to the Highlands and my love."

There it was again. Should he tell her to rethink Cavet? Angus ground his jaws together. No matter what he said, she wouldn't listen. She was young. In love. A lethal combination, and not one amenable to reason. In a burst of recklessness, he envied her all of it. He'd been young, but love had never been part of any equation with his name in it.

"Thank you," he said.

"For what?"

"Trusting me enough to talk with me."

"We'll be there soon," she said, bypassing his comment about trust.

"Aye, that we will. I was thinking we should request a special council meeting, so we can state our business."

"I wasn't planning to be that direct," she replied.

"If it was just you," he countered, "you might get away with wandering from cave to cave hunting a First Born, but I don't wish to tarnish the welcome I've always received from your kind."

The cadence of vibration in the tunnel shifted, announcing their imminent arrival in Fire Mountain. Angus waited. If Eletea were insistent about keeping a low profile, he wasn't certain what he'd do. There wasn't much chance of him sneaking into the dragons' homeworld undetected. He was about to point that out, when she eyed him, resigned.

"I'm not of a like mind, but we can do things your way. One of the things Cavet yelled at me about was I shouldn't have gone off on my own without his agreement. Pointing out he'd never have agreed bought me nothing."

"What are you saying?" Angus thought he knew, but wanted her to articulate it.

"Maybe a lesson I need to learn is how to play well with others— even when I know I'm right."

"Your strategy may be right for you, but it's not for me," Angus said, keeping his voice gentle, non-confrontational.

"Which is why I capitulated." The dragon clanked her jaws together. "You win, human. Don't rub it in."

"May I ask you a question?" He eyed her shrewdly, again almost certain of the answer, but thinking it would help her to hear it. At her nod, he went on. "Knowing the mess this created, would you do the same thing again?"

"Kill Mitha?"

"Aye."

A feral light kindled deep in her whirling eyes. "Of course I would. She's been so much trouble, I'm sorry I can't kill her twice."

Angus was still chuckling when the undulating gray-pink tunnel dissolved around them, and he walked out into the dragons' homeworld. It was a place of heat and light. Familiar smells—sulfur and ozone—buffeted him, singeing his lungs until he inhaled deeply, breathing past the pain. A charred landscape spread around them, beautiful in its barrenness. Red, orange, and black scorched dirt stretched in all directions.

Most of this land was a continuous string of volcanoes and lava flows ringed around caves. Dragons could go for long periods with no food and little water. Their few water sources lay hidden deep within extensive subterranean caverns. Though far from plentiful, it had always proven sufficient for the dragons and small herds of wildebeest-related ungulates they fed on.

Double suns dipped beneath the western horizon, turning the sky a deep crimson, like a bloody gash across the world. Soon the only light would be from the ever-present fires.

Eletea stretched to her full height of seven feet and spread her wings wider than she was tall. "It's so beautiful here," she murmured. "I forget as time passes."

Angus considered asking why she'd traded the desolation she found so appealing for the wet, misty Highlands, but remained silent.

She glanced at him. "I hate having anyone astride me, but you may as well jump on my back. It's a long walk to the caves where our council meets."

"I know where it is. I could use magic to get there."

Her eyes spun faster. "Get on. I won't ask again. Next time I'll blast you where I want you with dragons' fire. I already told you we're late."

Angus smothered a broad grin. He'd always wanted to ride a dragon. Even if they weren't going very far, it still thrilled him. He summoned power and vaulted to her broad back at the base of her neck. "Ready when you are."

"I'll just bet you are, human." Twisting, she blew smoke and steam in his face before she spread her wings and took off.

ARIANRHOD FIDGETED, waiting out the time it took to get to Fire Mountain. She wished there was an easier way, but this was the only road into the dragons' home. Not that dragons couldn't teleport in and out more directly, but no one else could. She redid the laces on her boots. Before she was quite finished with the second one, it was time to leave. She chanted the incantation to halt the time shaft, and it ejected her so harshly she landed on her stomach, splayed on red sand.

She sucked in a breath, followed by another. The hot, dry air stung, but it was better to dive in and move past the initial shock when it fried the delicate tissue lining her nose and throat. Thank Danu the suns were down, but volcanic fires that burned day and night kept this world from total darkness. She glanced about, taking her bearings. She never ended up the same place twice, probably a function of dragons manipulating when and where visitors showed up in their world.

As if to corroborate her theory, a golden dragon winged its way toward her, dropping lower by the moment. Since it was clear the dragon—no doubt the greeting party—was headed her way, she squared her shoulders and waited. It touched down a few feet away and lumbered toward her.

"Welcome moon goddess, goddess of the silver wheel, and virgin huntress."

The last words were devoid of inflection, but Arianrhod grimaced. Had rumors of her dalliance with Keene become common knowledge among dragonkind? She inclined her head.

"I'm afraid ye have me at a disadvantage. Ye know all my titles, but have yet to share any of yours."

"I am Kristel. No titles. I was sent to meet you and make certain you joined the other two who arrived earlier to address the same sorry business."

So much for pretending I'm considering becoming a dragon shifter.
Probably better this way.

"Aye, there are indeed two others I'm to meet here," she replied. "All of us were sent by Ceridwen, goddess of the world. We seek a First Born to settle a question of—"

Kristel rolled her eyes and snorted steam. "You humans are long on titles," she broke in. "And short on wisdom. The others are there." She pointed with a wingtip. "One league distant."

Arianrhod shrugged off annoyance at being interrupted and characterized as *human*. It wouldn't help, nor would it encourage the dragon to act differently. "Fine. 'Tis a lovely evening for a walk."

The dragon ground her double rows of teeth in a noise not unlike an angry buzz saw. "I was sent to escort you there."

"Excellent." Arianrhod shot a sunny smile her way. "Walk with me."

"Shut up and get on my back."

She didn't wait for a second invitation. Nothing compared with flying atop a dragon. Nothing. She'd enjoyed flying Keene as much as she enjoyed fucking him.

"Are we the only humans here?" she asked conversationally once she was mounted.

"We?" The dragon didn't bother to turn her head.

"Angus and I."

"Why would there be others?" The dragon flapped hard and vaulted into the air. Heat from her hide baked through Arianrhod's leathers. Between the air temperature and the dragon's warmth, she began to sweat.

"Don't mages still show up here in their quest to become dragon shifters?"

"We're rethinking that." Kristel did turn around then. Whirling green eyes settled on Arianrhod. "The bond brings far more to the mage than to the dragon. Mayhap 'tis time for us to refuse further supplicants."

Arianrhod schooled her features to neutrality. *Supplicants,* was it? Dragons were arrogant as hell. "The bond does make you immortal," she reminded Kristel.

"Eh, we live for thousands of years anyway. Not much of a selling point, particularly when it's balanced against our current spate of problems."

Arianrhod opened her mouth to say something conciliatory, but Kristel didn't give her a chance.

"I don't care if the mages shit gold to add to our hoards. They're not worth dragon turning against dragon. Danne is demanding Eletea's death. Eletea wants us to do some sort of exorcism on him. Her mate, Cavet, is yelling from the sidelines for us to snip Eletea's wings, so she doesn't escape his control again..." She stopped long enough to blow a gout of flame skyward in exasperation.

Arianrhod jumped into the breach. "I dinna realize your culture was patriarchal."

"What?" More flames. "It's not."

"Then what was that part about Eletea's mate wanting to control her every move?"

"That's just him. Hang onto the horns at the base of my neck. We'll be landing in a moment."

"Would ye put up with a male running things?" Arianrhod persisted. Her teeth clunked together when the dragon landed hard enough to rattle her spine. She called power and cushioned her journey to the ground. No reason to wait for further ire from a cranky dragon.

Kristel spun to face her. "Of course not. I plan to tell Eletea she should dump the bastard." She lowered her voice, breathing steam into Arianrhod's ear. "She's not his first mate. The other two ran screaming for Fire Mountain when he pulled that machismo crap with them."

Arianrhod cocked her head to one side. "What's the attraction?"

"He's gorgeous. Gold like me, but with golden eyes and quite a bit of, ahem, staying power."

"Sounds like ye've had some personal experience." Arianrhod smothered a knowing purr.

The dragon chuckled. "Yeah, he fucked bunches of us, but most had the good sense to leave it at that. Go through that opening in the mountainside. Another will guide you from there."

"Thanks for the ride." Arianrhod hefted her bow and quiver to a more stable position across her shoulders and strode forward.

"You're welcome. If you have a spot of free time, call for me. I do love a good gossip about our men." Her inflection was unmistakable. So the dragons did know about her and Keene. Not only knew, Kristel wanted to mine for details.

"Sure thing." Arianrhod waved cheerfully. Hell would turn to ice chips before she volunteered for another cozy chat with the dragon.

She ducked into the indicated opening, and breath caught in her throat. A large cave was lined with various sized mineral chunks, reflecting light from an unknown source. Teal, violet, pinks, and greens flickered in a kaleidoscopic display. Beautiful. She'd never seen anything to rival it.

While she stared, footsteps sounded in the distance, drawing near. She turned and for the second time in as many minutes, forgot to breathe. The man who materialized from shadow held such an ethereal presence, she wasn't certain he was real.

He glided toward her, a hand extended in greeting. "Arianrhod." His voice was deep, like rich whiskey, and she loved the sound of her name on his tongue. "I've heard so much about you. Nice we can finally meet."

She took his hand, and he closed it around her fingers, his grip warm, vibrant, sure. She knew she was staring, but couldn't help it. He was tall, maybe six-foot-four, with hair the color of old mahogany. It sheeted past his shoulders in silky waves. He had a high forehead, sharp cheeks, a beak of a nose, and a squared-off chin. Even though he wore nondescript clothes, they did nothing to disguise broad shoulders slabbed with muscle, a flat stomach, and slender hips. He sported knee-high lace-up boots similar to hers. Likely he had a hell of an ass, but she couldn't see that part of him. A few days' stubble dotted his cheeks and chin. Even with all that glory, his eyes were the best part. They reminded her of well-aged spirits, amber with golden flecks around the pupils.

He hadn't let go of her hand. Energy flowed into her, and she lapped it like nectar.

"Ye must be Angus." She swallowed back an inane desire to

giggle like a maid. "Since we're the only two with human form here, ye'd almost have to be."

"Good guess." His smile warmed his eyes. "Eletea and I have been here for a short time, and I was sent to guide you to the dragons' council chamber.

Self-conscious, she tugged her hand from his grip. It would never do to skip blithely into the Dragon Council holding hands like a couple of schoolkids. What if Keene was there?

So what if he is?

It's not as if he's made even the slightest effort to find me these past hundred years.

Color splotched Angus's face, and he glanced at his hand. "Sorry," he mumbled. "Didn't realize—"

She didn't bother telling him how difficult it was for her to sever their connection. Angus was stunning, but he'd been sent here by Ceridwen too. Which meant he lived much too close to home for her to consider smoothing her hands down that magnificent body and tangling them in all that wild, glorious hair.

"Which way?" She tossed a sunny smile his direction.

He smiled back shyly, and years fell away, making him look like a bashful boy, albeit a very hot one. "The way I came from." He rolled his eyes. "Nothing like stating the obvious, huh? Anyway, we should get going, the dragons are waiting for us—and keeping Danne and Eletea from scratching each other's eyes out."

"The dragon who brought me here said something about that. Apparently, Eletea has a mate who's cheering from the sidelines."

Angus frowned. "He doesn't want her dead, just—"

"Shuttling on a ball and chain between the bedroom and the kitchen," Arianrhod cut in.

Angus tossed his head back and laughed. The sound was velvety, masculine, and it sparked a reaction deep inside her. She wanted him to be joyful, yet she sensed resignation within him and wondered about its source.

"What you said about Cavet—that's Eletea's mate—about nailed it." Angus half bowed, a courtly, old-world gesture that made her smile. "This way. We probably shouldn't—"

A cacophony of dragon shrieks and screams blew through his words, obliterating the last of them.

Arianrhod had begun walking in the indicated direction, but she stopped dead. "Holy godhead. What the fuck do you suppose that's all about?"

"No idea, but it can't be good." He took off running, with her at his heels.

She readied magic, sensing she might need to kill something, and power was quicker than her bow. Besides, it'd be a neat trick to take down a dragon—even with a crossbow. Possible, but very difficult. Smoke billowed through the tunnel, making her eyes tear. Her lungs smarted from inhaling smoke, and she pitched into Angus's back because she couldn't see a thing in front of her.

"Ooph. Sorry," she panted and diverted a funnel of magic to clear the air enough to breathe. Dragons trumpeted around them, making her close to deaf as well as blind.

Angus waved a hand, and a bubble of clear air formed around them. "Better?" he asked, but she was coughing too hard to answer.

Black-tinged phlegm coated her hands where she'd coughed into them. "Yeah, thanks," she finally managed and wiped her palms on a nearby boulder.

He turned to face her and placed his mouth near her ear. "I tried calling for one of the dragons I spoke with earlier, but no one answered."

"I'm not surprised. No one could hear anything below eighty decibels in this racket."

A corner of his mouth twitched downward. "Good point. I'll try magic."

The murk darkened in front of them, and a green dragon lumbered close. "You!" the creature shrieked and pointed a talon at Angus. "If you'd come back sooner, none of this would've happened."

Arianrhod took a step forward. "If ye'd be so kind..." She inclined her head. "I need to know what we're dealing with."

"Why?" The dragon's dark eyes whirled ominously.

"So I can report back to Ceridwen—and the Morrigan." Arianrhod stood straighter, but was still feet shorter than the dragon. "Why else?"

"You'll do no such thing," the dragon retorted.

Arianrhod reined in a strong desire to roll her eyes. "What would ye suggest?" She was proud she kept sarcasm to a bare minimum. Not that it mattered. Dragons weren't that tuned into subtleties, and this one was so spun out, it would never notice.

"Since this is your doing, you'll be going after them." The dragon crossed its forelegs across its scaled chest.

"Going after whom?" Arianrhod ground her teeth together. "I'm facile at mindreading, but yours is closed to me." A lie. She hadn't bothered to look. The dragon was angry enough, it would've been be a waste of time.

"Danne and Eletea. Who else?"

"What happened? We need details if we're to do that," Angus cut in, his rumbly baritone infused with a compulsion spell.

Arianrhod wondered if the dragon would notice. Apparently not, because it showered them with steam that felt like being trapped in a very wet oven, and spat words with all the finesse of a freight train.

"Danne cast a spell far too strong for him. By the time I—and others—ascertained he had help, it was too late. Eletea and he had vanished."

Breath whistled from between Arianrhod's teeth. "Do ye mean to say he shanghaied her?"

"What I said was clear enough," the dragon pronounced.

Arianrhod peered through the murk with narrowed eyes. It was thinning, and the din of dragon shrieks had died down. "What are ye thinking we can do?" she demanded. "Doona dragons take care of their own?"

"Normally."

"You have to say more than that," Angus said. "I'll grant you this situation is anything but normal, yet I spent enough time with Eletea to sense her inner goodness. She's an honorable lass, er dragon. Why wouldn't you and your people go after Danne—and his accomplices, whoever they are?"

"This holds the stink of dragon shifter magic gone bad." The dragon pointed at them again and skewered Angus with his whirling gaze. "You can dream their location, and we believe you two will have a better chance of success locating them."

"I can't always control what information my visions yield," Angus protested.

"'Tis a fool's errand," Arianrhod cut in. "Eletea is probably already dead."

"If that's true, you'll return to tell us." Another puff of smoky steam.

"Have ye searched this world?" Arianrhod persisted, knowing she should hold her tongue, but unable to keep the words leashed within herself.

"They're not here, virgin huntress," the dragon sneered. "We're not so stupid as to send you on a *fool's errand*, no matter what you may think."

Arianrhod curled her hands into fists. There it was again. *Virgin.* She wanted to pound the arrogant dragon into a pile of cinders, scales, and gemstones, but she'd lose in any brand of combat— magical or otherwise.

The air in the bubble Angus had created around them shimmered oddly. When it cleared, they stood outside the cave in a night drenched by starlight.

Angus made a rude, very male noise somewhere between a grunt and a curse. "It would appear she dismissed us."

"No shit. How do ye ken the green was female?"

"Because I met all ten dragons who'd convened to create a council before I came to find you." He placed his hands on her shoulders and turned her to face him. "What do you wish to do, Arianrhod?"

"Why are ye asking me?"

He shrugged. "I figure you're a hell of a lot closer to Ceridwen than I'll ever be."

Something bitter, almost angry, ran beneath his words. She wanted to know more about it, but they had to leave Fire Mountain. And damned soon. Angus was correct about them being dismissed. Not simply sent away, but assigned a task on top of it. She still believed the dragons should take care of their own, but trotting back inside to promulgate her opinions would only piss the dragons off. She didn't want to end up barred from their world. Try explaining that to Ceridwen and the rest of her Celtic kinfolk.

Never mind the Morrigan.

"Likely I could dream the answers the Celts sent us to find," Angus said slowly, "but I hate to take the extra time. Eletea might still be alive, and it feels wrong to not begin hunting for her immediately."

"I'm not certain the problems aren't closely related," Arianrhod muttered. "Mayhap if we do the dragon's bidding, the rest of the picture will become clear. Sort of a *two birds with one stone* approach. We know Eletea killed the mage. What remains to be established is if the mage deserved killing."

"To hear Eletea's side of things, she did." Angus frowned. "What exactly are you considering? Ceridwen's expecting me back."

"Aye, and me as well, but keeping my kin waiting doesna bother me." She captured his gaze. "Once we find Eletea, the rest of the problem may well unravel for us."

His face lit with understanding. "Aye. I bet whoever helped Danne holds answers that dig deep into the dark mage problem."

"Precisely. Where'd your time portal spit you out?"

"Quite a way from here. We could conjure one, though, since you can enter and exit from any location in Fire Mountain. At least it'll hasten our departure."

She nodded and picked up the threads of a spell, pleased when he wove his magic seamlessly with hers. The shimmery, pearlescent maw of a traveling shaft split the ether in front of them, and he gestured her into it.

They'd been in motion for a short time when he asked, "Any idea what year to aim for?"

She barked a short, unfunny laugh. "Nay. Do ye?"

"Perhaps. Let's think this through. Danne's help likely came from the two dragons already corrupted by dark mages."

"How do ye know there are only two?"

He favored her with a grin that made him so handsome, she couldn't look away. "I don't. Eletea and I had ample opportunity for talk, and she mentioned Malik and Preki as problem dragons. There may be others."

"Do ye know the names of their mages?" Arianrhod closed her teeth over her lower lip and sent up a silent prayer they were men she'd heard of.

"That I do. Rhukon and Connor."

"Aye!" She punched the air with a closed fist. "I know them both." She bent over and checked a node that flashed by. "We'll aim for the late seventeen hundreds as a starting point."

"Excellent." His smile deepened. "We have a wee bit of time. Tell me what you know of the dragon shifter mages. If a vision comes, the more information I have, the better."

"Do your visions come often?" Curiosity burned bright, and she leaned closer.

"It depends. Sometimes they arrive unbidden, but more often I have to summon them." Warmth flared in the depths of his eyes. "Go ahead. I'm listening."

"Rhukon's castle used to be in Inishowen, and he had a manor house a few leagues south of Inverness, so he split his time between Ireland and Scotland. He was a fairly minor noble besotted with magic. It's unlikely either structure still stands in modern time, but we should have good luck in the late eighteenth century."

"What does he look like?" Angus bent toward her, interest stamped on his even features.

"Tall, heavily-muscled. Shoddy good looks. Dark brown eyes and midnight locks curling about his shoulders." She shrugged. "As I recall, he favored dandified clothing."

"I already don't like him. And the other one?"

"That's harder. Let me think." She rustled through her long memory. "Connor's never been known for his brilliance, yet in tandem with Rhukon, he does present a danger. His family is actually further up the food chain than Rhukon's in terms of money and power. Despite that, I never could figure out how he lured a dragon to bond with him. Generally dragons are smarter than that."

"Is he dark like Rhukon?"

She shook her head. "Nay. He has red-gold hair and blue eyes."

Angus chuckled.

"What's so funny?" Arianrhod cast a sidelong glance his way.

"They look like their dragons. Eletea told me Rhukon's was black and Connor's red."

"Never thought about it quite that way, but ye're right. In any event, Connor's people came from the Highlands, so we should aim for somewhere north of Fort William, at least as a starting point. If we get verra lucky, we'll find both Connor and Rhukon somewhere around Inverness."

"I live near there—in the twenty-first century—but I've been sent there to ferret things out from both the future and the past. It's interesting seeing the same place from different vantage points."

Arianrhod redirected her oblique gaze to face him more directly. "Are ye going to tell me more about that?"

"Nay." After a long pause, he added. "If you're truly curious, ask your kin."

She cocked her head to one side, intrigued. "Why them and not you?"

"I go where I'm sent. Like right now. If I had my way, I'd be swimming with the Selkies off Northern Ireland."

Her interest deepened. "Selkies is it? What exactly are you?"

"I have no idea."

The bitterness she'd picked up earlier was back in force. She considered scanning him with magic to answer her own question, but restrained herself. Instead, she picked a different approach. "How is it ye doona know?"

"Arawn fished me from a time-travel tunnel when I wasn't much past boyhood. He did something, so I have no memories from before then. If I had a place to return to, I have no idea where or when it is." He hooded his gaze.

Arianrhod shuttered her magic to offer the illusion of privacy in their cramped quarters. Obviously the god of the dead had his reasons for waylaying Angus. Arawn never did anything that wasn't carefully scripted beforehand. She ground her teeth together in frustration. He and Gwydion were two of a kind. Magic pushed against her mind. She took a chance and laid a hand on Angus's thigh.

He flinched and said, "Don't. I don't want your pity."

"I wasna offering pity. Ye do want my knowledge, or ye wouldna have tried to peek inside my head just now."

He looked hard at her, his eyes on fire with resentment. "Wouldn't you do damn near anything to find out who you are? What you're capable of?" The line of his jaw tightened. "Maybe since you've always known those things, you can't imagine what it's like to discover power you had no idea you possessed. Except you're clumsy with it when it first surfaces."

Once he began talking, his voice rose, and words came faster. "No one's ever given me a straight answer—about anything. Some of what I dream is true-seeing, some isn't. I've handed over information that created enormous problems."

"Och, it canna be as bad as all that." She tried for diplomacy, shielding her kin and hating herself for misplaced loyalty.

"Yeah, it can." Muscles rippled across his jaw as he engaged in an inner struggle she could only guess at. "Your brother and some of the others have killed innocents on the basis of my visions."

"Mayhap they doona know any more than you—" The words tasted false on her tongue, so she cut them off. "Why do ye suppose Arawn hid your origins? What of the others who tapped you to do their bidding? Even though we've never met afore, I've heard your name bandied about."

"If I knew the answers to any of that, I wouldn't be here."

"Have ye tried telling them no?"

A short bark of a laugh, so harsh the tunnel walls drew back, burst from him. He twisted his mouth into a wry expression. "Have you ever told Ceridwen no?"

"Touché. Only on verra rare occasions. I've thought about it frequently, mind ye, but I'm one of them. Loyalty among brothers and all that rot. Ye should have a shred more latitude."

"It seems I have far less. No say in anything, except during the brief periods when no one wants me to play whipping boy for them."

"I'm sorry."

His already intense gaze bored into her. She dropped her shielding and allowed him free access to her mind. It was a risk, but a small one. If he wished her ill, she'd have sensed it.

"You're telling the truth." Incredulity underscored his words, and he withdrew from her mind.

"Aye. Of course I am. What would be the purpose in lying to you?"

"I don't know." He laid a hand over the one she still had on his upper leg. "I'm so used to the Celts playing me like their own personal puppet, it never occurred to me you wouldn't be like all the rest."

Och, sweetheart. If ye only knew...

"Perhaps I can help figure out who ye are."

"Why would you do that?" He forged on without stopping for breath. "If Arawn and Ceridwen and the rest found out, they'd be furious. The only reason I keep dancing to their tune is because they dangle the truth of my beginnings in front of me like a piece of meat before a starving dog. Part of me doesn't give a crap anymore, but another part does."

Outrage filled her mouth with a bitter taste. Her kin had used him—were still using him. She set her jaw in a determined line. "It appears ye've figured out they'll never say aught, yet ye still capitulate. Why?"

Color swept from the open neck of his shirt to his tanned cheeks. "I ask myself that every single time one of the Celts shows up with a new chore."

"Have ye come up with an answer?" She kept her tone soft, non-confrontational.

He tightened his hand atop hers. "Aye, but I'm not proud of it. I'm afraid of what they'd do to me, how they'd punish me if I defied them." He straightened his spine. "There are other reasons too. You asked about my visions. I have no life of my own for the best of reasons. I fall into dreams, deep trances where I'm helpless." He stopped, and an uncomfortable look washed across his face. "What I dream almost always comes to pass."

Pieces clicked into place. She tried to rein in her reaction, but didn't do a very good job. No wonder Arawn strung him along and likely kept an open link to his mind. The dragon suggested Angus could dream the truth, and he'd mentioned trance states, but she hadn't put the information together.

Until now.

He gripped her chin with his other hand and forced her to look at him. "Tell me," he demanded, his voice rough. "Tell me what you know."

CHAPTER 5

She pulled away from his grasp and bent to examine a node as it passed, more to buy time to consider what to do next than anything else. Surprise flared when she understood they needed to exit—and very soon. "We'll talk more once we're out of here," she said, and summoned power to slow the shaft's undulations so they could leave.

"You figured something out," he persisted. "I felt it."

The time-travel shaft shuddered to a halt, and one of its walls opened onto a thick, evergreen forest. "Aye, 'tis true," she said, "but we must leave. Now."

He followed her into a driving rain, blinking water from his eyes. "At least the weather hasn't changed in the last two hundred fifty years," he muttered.

She wished for one of her stout, woolen, hooded cloaks, rather than the leather she wore. Behind them, a jolt in the damp air told her the traveling shaft had winked out of existence. She started to mark the spot in her mind, but didn't bother. Magic was much closer to the surface here than in modern time. They could conjure a portal from damn near anywhere, just like they'd done on Fire Mountain.

Angus pushed magic into a rough circle around them and pointed north. "Inverness is that way. And not all that far. Which side are we aiming for?"

A dragon's shrill hunting cry split the soggy air, and she pulled invisibility about them both. "Damn it!" She kept her voice low, made it blend with the rain sounds.

"Solves one problem."He moved to her side, and she restructured her ward.

"Which one would that be?" she inquired acidly.

"They're expecting someone to come after Eletea, which likely means they've set traps." He shook wet hair back from his face. "They went to a lot of trouble to kidnap her. Not a big surprise, they'd guard their prize well."

"I'm not seeing which problem that particular piece of knowledge solves." Arianrhod smothered irritation. "Fuck this whole mess. Let Ceridwen find other flunkies."

"Nay. Not a good idea. We're here. We must help Eletea, and the most important task is maintaining the element of surprise."

"How do ye know the dragon that passed overhead dinna spot us?"

"A hunch." He smiled, and water dripped off his nose. "If it had, do you believe it would've left?"

"Mmph. Probably not. May as well get moving. As I recall, shepherds' huts dot the hillsides in this area. Mayhap we'll be fortunate and find an empty one where we can dry out and craft a plan."

"I can do you one better." Angus's grin widened. "There's an empty manor house not far from here." He started off at a quick pace and turned to glance back at her. "Coming? Or should I draw my own invisibility casting?"

Arianrhod hurried after him, still sunk in ambivalence. She didn't want to get sucked into the Celtic chaos that would blow up in her face if she disclosed her suspicions about Angus's origins to him. Beyond that, resentment simmered that she was back in the

Age of Reason, never one of her favorite time periods. People knew just enough then to become dangerous, plus it spawned the beginning of problems that would cause the eventual downfall of Earth's fragile ecosystems.

Focus! Her inner voice held a sharp edge.

Fortunately, Angus wasn't inclined toward conversation as she trudged through thick, muddy undergrowth behind him. It was easier than cutting her own path, and she wanted to keep expenditure of magic to a bare minimum—in case more dragons flew overhead.

She eyed his broad shoulders and considered coming up with a well-crafted lie, swathed in enough illusion to fool him, but she couldn't convince herself to become the latest Celt in a long string to screw him over.

Angus deserved to hear what she was fairly certain was the truth about himself. Damn Arawn anyway. And her brother, Gwydion. And Ceridwen, who had to be in on the deception. They must've had need of Angus to go to all that trouble. She also understood why they'd kept their mouths shut. Angus would've returned to his own time and his own people—if he knew who they were.

That her kin had held him here, working for them, was unconscionable. Yet if she blew the lid off everyone's maneuverings, the Pantheon would turn on her. Was it worth being targeted?

Of course not. It's why I've kept my sex life off their radar.

She pitched against Angus's back for the second time that day. "Och. Sorry. Wasna paying attention."

"I figured as much." He gestured in front of them through more trees. "The place I had in mind isn't far. I stopped so we might determine if it's still uninhabited."

She wanted to ask when he'd stumbled across it. Instead, she focused a thin stream of power in the direction he indicated, careful to keep it subtle. "Looks good to me," she said after scanning twice.

"Aye, I found the same, but wanted confirmation." He shook himself, and droplets flew in all directions. "I'm not sure we have the time, but we need to think things through." Shrewd amber eyes drilled into her. "If I have magic that could turn things in our favor, I need to know that too."

She winced. There it was. He wasn't going to let things lie, but then she'd known that from the moment he gripped her chin in the time shaft.

He bent so his mouth hovered near her ear. "I'd never tell where the information came from."

"It doesna matter. They'd know. Besides, the best strategy with my kin is facing things head on." She straightened her spine. "Lead out. I think better when rain isna dripping down my neck."

An odd look crossed his face, cynicism warred with anger. "*Head on* may be your strategy. No one's bothered to employ it with me."

She didn't waste words apologizing for the other Celts again. It wouldn't change anything.

They cleared the last band of trees and came into a clearing no one had maintained for quite some time. Bushes pushed their way beyond the forest's edge, and weeds grew thickly up to the gray stone walls of a manor house. From the feel of things, it had been deserted for many years. She glanced upward, counting five stories. The place was huge, but falling into disrepair, with stones missing from the walls. Ivy clustered thickly, maybe the primary thing holding the walls in place. She could only imagine what sort of shape the roof was in, but it shouldn't matter, so long as they stuck to the lower floors.

Angus led her to a door mostly sunk into the ground and pushed it inward with a combination of magic and strength. "Careful," he said. "This was the kitchen entrance, and steps are missing toward the bottom."

She followed him, ending up in a corridor lit only by daylight from the open doorway. Arianrhod summoned a mage light and sent a small jolt of power to pull the door shut behind them. She added to her spell and obliterated evidence of their presence outside the manor house.

Angus was already moving away from her. He opened one of many doors off the corridor, and she shadowed him up stone steps and into an enormous room with fireplaces sunk into the wall at one end. Mice and rats scattered, heading back to wherever they lived when they weren't cruising for food.

He stood in a doorway at the far end of the kitchen. "We need a smaller room," he said. "Something easier to warm with magic, since fire's not a good idea."

Many doors and hallways later, he ushered her into a small, cozy parlor. Other than dust, the space seemed untouched by whatever had ravaged the remainder of the manor. She closed the door behind them and shucked her bow and quiver, laying them on an oaken side table. Even without deploying magic of her own, she understood.

"You spelled this room." She brushed dust off a padded chair and sat on it.

"That I did. I haven't been here for a while, but I spent enough time in this era, I needed a place I didn't have to work on every time they sent me here." He paused for a beat. "You didn't ask, but I checked for Eletea's energy while we were heading here. She's still alive—very much so if the outrage spilling from her is any indication."

Arianrhod chided herself. She should've done the same thing, but hadn't. Of course it was easier for Angus, since he had the feel of the dragon's energy, whereas she'd need to sort through many different dragon emanations, hoping she guessed right. Bending over, she wrung water out of her hair and set to work braiding it to keep it out of the way.

Angus dragged a chair over with one sodden boot and sat across from her. He didn't say a word, just waited. The expression on his face—eager, hopeful, resigned, cynical—caught her heartstrings in a vise.

"How's your mythology?" She quirked a brow and continued to

work on her hair. Because it came to her feet, it took a long time to gather the silvery strands into braids.

"Fair." He scrunched his face into a smile that lit his eyes from within. "You can answer questions if I have any."

"Aye, that would be true." She flipped the first of what would be four braids over one shoulder and went to work on the next section of hair. Either she told him—or she didn't. There wasn't any middle ground. Her earlier idea to feed him a half-truth didn't play well. She had to live with herself afterward, and the look in his eyes would haunt her forever as it was.

"Waiting won't make it any easier."

"Nay, probably not." She stopped with half her hair finished. "Do ye mind if I look inside you? 'Twill either support what I suspect, or it may yield something I dinna anticipate."

"You have my permission," he said, suddenly solemn.

She understood. He'd wanted this forever, but what if he couldn't live with the answers?

Assuming I find something. Right now all I have is speculation tempered with some old stories. Mayhap true, but just as likely not.

She got to her feet and walked to him. "I'm going to place a hand on either side of your head. Doona fight me."

He pushed his shoulders back and nodded sharply.

She took her time, gentle as she sorted through layers of ensorcellment no doubt placed by her kin, snipping strands as she went. She thought she recognized Gwydion's handiwork. Ceridwen's too. It had been important to whoever created the magical shielding that Angus not stumble onto the truth by accident.

When she was as certain as she was likely to get, she withdrew and exhaled in a *whoosh.*

"That bad?" Determination tightened his features into a mask. He clearly wanted to know what she'd found—no matter what it was.

Concern smote her, and she sank to the floor next to him. "Nay.

Nothing like that. I found what I expected." She stopped, hunting words. "'Tisn't bad, yet I'm not sure quite what the knowledge will buy you. Ye're descended from Cathbad and Nessa, mayhap their son, mayhap a grandson."

His eyes widened, and he drew back. "The Druid seer and his one-time Irish royal consort?"

"Aye. It appears your mythology is sharper than ye led me to believe. Although Nessa was daughter to Eochaid Sálbuide, king of Ulster, ye're close enough."

Angus drew his brows together. "I don't understand. Why hide that from me? It's harmless enough."

"Because I suspect someone—mayhap Arawn, mayhap another of us—drew you from your time into ours. They clouded your memories and wound layer upon layer around your mind, so ye woudna ever discover your origins."

"They figured I'd demand to be returned, eh? Or that I'd hunt down someone who could demand it on my behalf."

"That's my guess," she replied.

He pushed still-wet hair away from his face. "Their son, Nessa's and Cathbad's, was Conchobar. Right?" At her nod, he went on. "It would be easy enough to discover if he disappeared."

"Aye, that it would." She looked up at him and grasped one of his wrists. "A man needs to know who he is, yet what would that buy you?"

"Probably not much, yet it would give me a place to return. Whether I am Conchobar or his son or grandspawn."

"Ye could've left any time," she said gently. "When Arawn went after you—and I suspect he did so for a reason—ye were verra young. Now ye're a man. Arawn, Gwydion, even Ceridwen couldna harm you. Not anymore."

He gazed at her. "The magic you drilled through, whatever was swathed around my mind, it's gone now. I know because I feel… different. Clearer, more confident, like I could be whole again."

"And?" She gazed back, losing herself in the magic of his eyes.

He didn't answer. Instead, he slid to the floor next to her and gathered her into his arms. She nestled against him. The beat of his heart kindled longing in her blood, but she held back. He might be grateful to her, nothing more. Sex was such a minefield. What she'd done by clearing his memories and opening his heritage to him was bad enough. To compound it with sex would mean she'd truly never be welcomed by her kin again.

She could try to hide what she'd done. Maybe she'd get away with it for a while, but they'd find out eventually—about her loose tongue and the sex.

Do I care?

What have any of them ever done for me?

Angus smoothed the loose half of her hair back over her shoulders. "You have the most beautiful hair," he murmured. "When the light plays over it, it's like spun silver, but with golden flecks that come alive. And your eyes. One gold, the other silver. I've never seen the like, and gods know I've spent enough time among the Celts."

"What do ye know about me?" She cuddled closer, loving the hard planes of his body against hers. Before she could think better of the idea, she wrapped her arms around him. Wet wool met her fingertips, covering the body beneath. A body she desperately wanted to see and touch and taste.

"What do I know of you?" Gentle humor underscored his words. "You're the Moon-Mother Goddess. Because the moon descends into the sea, you also rule the tides and Caer Sidi, a magical realm to the north."

"Long ago," she murmured, her words nearly lost against the crook between his neck and shoulder. "All that was long ago. Men now, they doona worship gods or goddesses. 'Tis been many a long year since I've thought of the moon or Caer Sidi."

"Surely your magical realm remains." He cupped her neck in one long-fingered hand and rubbed the tense places.

"I doona know," she said. "Magic requires belief."

"I believe in you." He shifted her in his arms, gazed at her for long moments before closing his mouth over hers.

She thought she should turn away. He gave her opportunity. His kiss was gentle, demanding nothing of her. He was offering her a choice. The deep loneliness she lived with every day of her immortal existence bubbled up, choking her with the specter of more days, weeks, months, and years alone.

All of them.

Or none, if she followed her heart.

She threaded her hands beneath his rough-cut mahogany hair and pushed her tongue inside his mouth.

He moaned low in his throat, and the gentleness in his kiss vanished, replaced by a need so primal and fierce, it stole her breath.

CHAPTER 6

$\mathcal{A}$ngus felt her indecision, knew when it shifted to desire as urgent as his own. Recognition flared that she had wounded places, regret that ran far deeper than his since she'd lived so much longer.

Or had she? Now that he had some inkling of his origins, how long had he lived?

He didn't want to think about the unknowns that plagued him. Not with her in his arms. She'd given him a gift, an unexpected windfall. He'd sort through what the knowledge meant later.

The lithe body pressed against him held great power and great longing. She was supposed to be the virgin huntress, yet she was no maid, not if he were any judge of such things.

Angus teased her mouth with his tongue. She tasted sweet, like summer wildflowers or well-aged brandy. Arianrhod gave herself to their kiss, melting into his arms as if she'd been born to be a part of him. Her nipples pebbled where her breasts pressed against his chest.

He wanted everything. To see her, taste her, run his tongue and fingers all over her magnificent body. She bit his lower lip, and he nipped back, making a low moan of need bubble from her throat. Or maybe it was he who made the sound.

She tore her mouth from his and moved her hands around his body, where she slid them beneath his worn, woolen top. Once it had been a rich, dark blue, but it had faded to gray in some spots, pale blue in others. Her hands lit a fire beneath his skin, and he worked at the lacings holding her leather top in place. Frustrated when the knots didn't yield, he pulled her top up to expose her breasts.

Breath clotted in his throat as he stared at the firm globes tipped by golden nipples.

She laughed deep and low. "Ye doona have to worship me. I'd much rather ye did more than look."

Yearning filled him so full, his erect cock was the least of it. He tumbled both her breasts into his hands and bent his head to take a nipple into his mouth. It hardened still more beneath his questing tongue, and he sucked until a sharp, gasping breath told him there was far more of her to explore. The body beneath his hands and tongue held magic, power. Her milky skin glowed with an inner light as if she were on fire. Just like the dragons.

Just like him.

Arianrhod tangled her hands in his hair and pulled him away from her breasts. "Let me undress you."

"What if I want to do the same to you?" He was surprised he could get words past his tongue, which felt stuck to the roof of his mouth.

She pushed her top back down, undid the laces with a cunning twist of her hands and pulled the soft leather over her head. Next, she tugged his shirt out of the way. It was still heavy with rainwater. She tossed it over a nearby chair and chanted something. Vapor rose from it, and he understood she was drying it for him.

He made a grab for her breasts again, but she shook her head and wriggled downward until she was next to his laced boots. "Turn around," he commanded. "I'll get yours off at the same time." His fingers weren't quite as uncooperative as his tongue when he attacked the laces.

Once he had her boots and stockings in a heap off to one side, he moved back to where he could circle her slender waist with both hands and bent to string kisses from her breasts lower to her flat belly, still covered by her clothing. Someone, maybe him, maybe her, made short work of the leather lacing that held her breeches in place. The intoxicating scent of her engulfed him as he pushed her pants down her legs, followed by smallclothes of finely milled, ivory silk.

She writhed beneath his grip, back bowed with desire and head thrown back. He could've gazed at her for hours. She was the apex of everything female. Beautiful, desirable, and soon, very soon, his. He moved his mouth back to her stomach and kissed his way down to tight, silver curls guarding the entrance to her sex. His hands found their way under her glorious ass, and he held her before him, breathing on her, teasing her with the rolled tip of his tongue.

Her hips bucked toward his mouth, and he settled his lips over her nub, sealing them around her engorged flesh. As he sucked, he slid a hand between her legs and pressed two fingers inside her body. Muscles clutched him, and he worked her between his mouth and fingers until rhythmic contractions and a low, keening moan told him she was coming.

She buried her hands in his hair and held him against her, twisting and squirming until her pleasure settled.

"I want you inside me." Her voice was rough, harsh with needing him, and she jackknifed her body out from under his and tackled the buttons that held his trousers closed. He was so lost in rut, it didn't occur to him to help until she pushed his pants down enough to extract his cock.

"Magnificent!" She ran a fingertip from the base of his penis to its tip and cast a coquettish glance his way. "How many girls back home are standing in line for this?" She caressed him again, and her touch ignited a depth of longing he'd only dreamed of.

"Just one, and she's a Selkie." He slithered out of his pants and turned back to her. "Tell me how to please you."

"Ye already please me. More than anyone has in a verra long time." Her eyes twinkled, and she rubbed a clear drop of semen around the head of his cock. It jerked in her grasp, urging him to move beyond talking.

He pulled a pillow off one of the couches and lay on the floor, tucking the pillow beneath his head. His cock jutted out from his body, and he wrapped a hand around his shaft. He gestured with the other, and she understood. Tossing a leg over him, she straddled him and lowered her body slowly over his waiting cock. She made small, eager sounds, punctuated with Gaelic, as his girth stretched her. He steadied her with a hand on her hip until he was fully encased in the heat of her body. She rocked and tightened herself around him.

Pleasure flooded his senses, cutting a broad path from his toes to the top of his head. He joined her in small movements, teasing, getting to know her body. Sensation, sharp and urgent, prodded like a thousand tiny flames. He reached for her pussy and rubbed her clit. She covered his hand with hers, showing him what she wanted. Tension ratcheted in the slick tissue surrounding him. Her breathing quickened, and she swirled her hips around his shaft, deepening the delight that grew between their bodies.

He withdrew all the way and drove himself into her, no longer satisfied with teasing. They needed the real thing, coupling as bawdy and vital as anything Aphrodite, Pan, or the Satyrs could imagine. Her breasts bounced above him, their nipples tight buds of desire. Her clit hardened and lengthened beneath his questing fingers.

When he felt the flutters in her body that signaled her release and heard her cry out, he let go of any semblance of control. Semen boiled at the base of his balls and juddered from him in white-hot gouts. She dug her fingers into his shoulders, and he felt her come again, quivering around him as she yielded to the craving that bonded them.

He'd never wanted a woman as much as he wanted the one in his arms. Not that he'd spent very much of his life fucking, but the desire he'd felt before was a pale, pallid thing compared with what ran through his veins now.

"Aye, I feel it too," she murmured, and he knew she'd been inside his head. For a moment, he felt embarrassed, but pushed it aside.

"I'd love to spend hours with you." He placed his hands on her arms and pulled her down on top of him.

"We canna tarry further. We must find Eletea," she said, her voice garbled because her head lay on his shoulder, and her face was buried against his neck.

He cradled her in his arms and rubbed his hands down the length of her shapely back. "Once we're done, we can find more time for each other."

Her skin, so supple a moment before, flinched beneath his touch. "'Twas a risk I took with you just now," she said. "We shall see what the future brings." Arianrhod extricated herself from his embrace and pushed herself upright until she sat beside him, gazing at him through troubled eyes.

"What?" he asked. A cold tongue of fear curdled the joy he'd felt moments before.

Bitterness to rival his own twisted her perfect face into something unattractive. "A while back, I asked if ye knew who I was. Ye gave me part of the story, yet some is missing." She took a deep breath and blew it out. "I'm the virgin huntress. *Virgin*. It means I doona couple with men—or anyone else."

Understanding pounded jagged claws into him. He'd finally found a woman he might love, not just one to share sex with like Celene, and she wasn't available. The light he'd allowed to grow inside him guttered and went out. He got to his feet and gathered pieces of clothing, hurriedly donning them.

Arianrhod did the same. She looked embarrassed, or maybe the color highlighting her skin was left over from their lovemaking. She reached for her quiver and bow, but stopped and made a point of facing him squarely.

"Angus."

He didn't particularly want to listen to her rationalizations, so he shook his head. "You don't have to say a word. I get it. What happened between us was a onetime deal." Because he couldn't control his mouth, it curled into a harsh line. "Don't worry. I won't blow your cover."

Anger flashed from her multicolored eyes. "That's not it." She fisted a hand and drove it into her open palm. "I dinna ask for my role in the Pantheon, yet I'm stuck with it. As ye've figured out, I've scarcely kept my part of the bargain. In my own way, I'm just as isolated and lonely as ye are."

He tightened his jaw into a tense line. This was getting worse and worse. "So what just happened between us was a pity fuck? Because you feel sorry for me and yourself?"

Arianrhod shook her head and shrank into herself. "Nay. 'Tisn't what I'm saying at all. Och, but I'm making a botch of this." She drew her silver brows together. "Mayhap what I want to say is ye're beautiful. I wanted exactly what happened. Ye in my arms and inside my body. It was amazing, better than my best imaginings, yet I fear we borrowed pleasure from a place that charges high interest." She tossed her shoulders back and tilted her chin defiantly. "Once we're done here, we must return to our own time. Me to my charade of an existence, and ye to however ye wish to address your problem with my kinfolk."

She walked to him and placed a hand on the side of his face. "'Tis all right if they know I told you of your origins. The minute ye disclose what ye know, they'll likely realize it came from me, and I'll defend your right to that knowledge before our council. Our compact with men forbids what they did to you.

"They'll argue ye're not exactly a man, but that's semantics."

He frowned, anger draining from him as he listened. "I could go back to wherever they dragged me from."

"Ye could—and we may well do so—but ye may not find what ye seek. Magical intervention rarely works that way."

Angus considered her words, hunted for a frame of reference for them. "In our time, modern time, only twenty-five years have passed since Arawn hauled me from that time-travel shaft. Things can't have shifted quite so much."

Arianrhod nodded. "Ye just said the magic words: *time-travel shaft*. Ye traveled through time, no doubt for a purpose that was scrubbed from your memory. 'Tis been over a thousand years since Nessa and Cathbad walked the Earth. Even if ye're grandchild from that mating, or great-grandchild, ye may not find them. I could be mistaken, but I doona believe Cathbad or Nessa held the keys of immortality."

He sifted his hands through his hair. None of this was easy or straightforward. "I need to consider my actions carefully," he murmured.

"Only a fool doesna do so." She favored him with a smile that smote his heart. "And ye're far from a fool." She tightened the hand that still cupped his cheek. "I would things were different, yet they're not."

Because he couldn't stand to not say the words, because they raged within him, he caught her gaze and held it. "This topic isn't closed. We'll talk more once we've dispatched the problem of Eletea and the rogue dragon shifters who abducted her."

A tiny smile flitted about Arianrhod's mouth. "Mayhap we shall. I'm weak where ye're concerned. Were I wise, I'd tell you nay. We've said all we need to, yet wanting you burns within me, twin flame to what smolders in you."

Hope surged, but Angus tamped it down and wound wards around his mind so she couldn't see in. There had to be a way. At least she wasn't closed to the possibility. For now, it would have to be enough.

~

Arianrhod slung her quiver over her shoulder and followed it with her bow. Part of her was furious she hadn't taken a stronger stand, but she couldn't shut the door on the man walking ahead of her. She was so lost in thought, she missed a turn and had to double back to find the way they'd come in.

Her clothes were drier, but the leather felt clammy until her body warmed it. She should've spelled her breeches and jerkin to dry as she'd done with his shirt. After making her way up the steep, broken stairwell, she stepped outside. At least the rain let up, but night had fallen while they were inside. Thick clouds obscured both moon and stars, so she called a mage light into being. It burned a soft violet next to her, and would follow like an obedient puppy when they set off. She felt hungry, but food would have to wait. They shouldn't have indulged themselves with sex; further delay to hunt and cook game would be inexcusable.

"I agree. Not about sex being a mistake, but about there not being time to scare up a meal." He moved behind her, clearly having helped himself to her thoughts.

She slapped up wards. Much as she wanted Angus in every way a woman could want a man, it wasn't good for them to be joined at the hip. Sharing thoughts would only deepen the bond thrumming between them. She'd have to make a clean cut, cleave straight through it, but maybe not quite yet.

Coward. What a filthy coward I am.

She turned toward him and stilled her jumbled mind. "I say we head for Rhukon's castle. 'Tisn't far from here."

"Are we going to waltz up to the front door and knock?" He quirked a brow her way.

"Nay." She furled her brows back at him. "We shall use stealth and cunning. All the old castles had a network of underground passageways."

"In case the lord of the manor needed to make a quick getaway?"

"Aye. Other reasons as well. More often than not, he also needed a way to sneak his collection of women—or pretty men—in and out."

"I see." Angus snorted soft laughter, then quieted. "We'll need to be very careful. We're more likely to find dragons than maids beneath Rhukon's castle."

"I agree. We could use magic to transport us closer, but walking is safer."

He made a mock, sweeping bow that almost planted his forehead on the wet ground. "After you. I sense Eletea, but beyond that I have no idea what Rhukon's place looks like."

Arianrhod nodded to herself. "Let me send you an image. I canna be killed, but in the unlikely event I'm knocked unconscious, at least ye'll recognize it."

"Thanks. Mmph. Another old, crumbling stone mausoleum. Not sure I would've liked living in this time." He looped an arm around her shoulders and walked by her side.

"Buildings were much more primitive in the time you came from." She thought about ducking from beneath his embrace, but his warmth by her side felt solid, exciting, and right in a way not much else had in her long life.

"Forget about architecture. We need our own dragon," he said.

"Why? They're impossible to hide."

"I wasn't looking at it that way." He chuckled. "We'll be impossible to hide once we get close. We can mask ourselves, but the moment we do something useful, we'll give our position away."

"What would a dragon do for us?" She grinned and leaned closer to him.

"We could make a grand, aerial entrance. None of this cloak and dagger crap. And it would give us an ally—in case the dragon shifters take us on in beast form."

Arianrhod sobered fast. "Ye'd best hope they doona do that. If they do, escaping from here with our hides intact will become verra difficult. Along those lines, if I tell you to leave, ye will do so. They willna harm me, mostly because they canna, but they might kill you."

He stopped walking and swung her to face him. "I'm not leaving you to face danger by yourself. It's not up for discussion, so don't waste your breath. Besides…" A crooked grin lit his austere features. "I may be immortal."

"Unlikely, besides we canna count on that. Are ye always this stubborn?" She swept the unbraided half of her hair over a shoulder.

Something deep in his whiskey-colored eyes melted. "Aye, but only when something I care deeply about is on the block."

Her mouth twitched into a reluctant smile. "Ye make me sound like a prize pig up for auction."

"If you are, then you're my prize pig."

Before she could protest, he covered her mouth with his and kissed her long and deep. She felt herself falling, losing her grip on who she needed to be. Arianrhod wrenched her mouth from his.

"We shouldna."

"Too late. We already have." He cut off further words with another kiss.

She kissed him back because she couldn't bear not to, and snaked her arms around him, splaying her hands across his back. Nothing else mattered but his mouth on hers, his arms around her, and his body crushed against hers.

CHAPTER 7

Dragons trumpeting from above forced reality back into focus, and Arianrhod pulled away from Angus at the same time she draped invisibility about them, hoping she wasn't too late. She peered upward, but the skies were dark and silent. When she next heard the dragons—at least two of them—they'd moved away.

"No more kissing." She shook a finger at Angus. "We have a task. Ye addle my mind."

"It's good for you. And certainly, it's good for me. I've followed orders like the lowest form of hired help for far too long."

She didn't want to get drawn into a conversation she'd be prone to agree with. Arianrhod narrowed her eyes. "Can ye still sense Eletea?"

"Of course. If her life force had ebbed at all, we'd be on our way to rescue her. As it is, we lost nothing these last few moments when my lips sought yours."

Arianrhod smothered a laugh. Men. Silken-tongued, single-minded. Except in this instance, she wanted the man in question as desperately as he wanted her.

"How many dragons do you recall from this era?"

She considered the question before she answered. "Hard to say. Dragons left Fire Mountain with greater frequency a couple hundred years ago. Sometimes they came here; sometimes they traveled to one of the borderworlds. Are ye asking to determine if the ones in the sky were Malik and Preki?"

"Exactly. If they were, then Rhukon and Connor are in shifted form."

She blew out a breath. "Since they must take one form or the other—man or dragon—that makes sense. But we doona know which dragons were in the sky."

"Can we use magic to find out?"

"Nay. If we did, they'd be on us in a trice. Dragons are very sensitive to all variations of power directed their way."

He crinkled his forehead in thought. "Best get moving toward where I sense Eletea. Once we lay eyes on where she's being held, we can determine what to do next."

Arianrhod fell into step next to him, taking care to guard them from prying eyes and ears.

"Can you kill a dragon?" His deep voice rumbled near her ear.

"Not the dragon shifters. Immortality is part of the bargain. The others, aye, but 'tis verra difficult. What are ye thinking of doing?"

"Unless Danne had a change of heart and isn't here, our best bet would be to knock him out of the picture."

She pushed her tongue against her teeth. Killing dragons went against the grain, no matter what they'd done. The ancient creatures were arrogant and a pain in the ass, but they were a miracle too. "Mayhap we can find another way."

"Like what?" He grabbed her arm. "Slow down. It's not far." He batted at a thick, evergreen branch that doused them with water when he touched it. "Wish I could see something, but between the night and the trees, it's not easy."

"I muted my mage light because—"

"I know why you did that," he broke in. "It's the same reason I didn't kindle my own. Ssht." He slunk forward, his magic muffled down to nothing.

She did what she could to hide them and wove her energy with his. They stopped at the edge of a large clearing, but remained under the thick forest canopy. Arianrhod knew this place. Rhukon's manor house rose through the foggy gloom. Six floors of rough-hewn timbers, huge river rocks, and mortar holding everything together—more or less. Lanterns burned from some windows, but most of the structure was dark, which made sense. Pre-electricity, people used illumination sparingly, choosing to sleep through the dark hours.

"She's underneath the house." Angus spoke into her mind.

"Good news." Arianrhod turned in a full circle. She kept her magic subtle as she searched for what had to be there: a subterranean way inside that didn't involve using any of the obvious entrances. When her first scan yielded nothing, she tried again, altering the frequency of her search. Modern life was good for some things; radio waves didn't exactly mimic magical emanations, yet some similarities existed, and they'd enriched how she manipulated her own abilities.

Angus threaded his arm around her and blended tendrils of power with hers. It was enough of a boost, she found what she sought.

"This way." She motioned, and they faded deeper into the forest. Magical antennae on high alert, she came to a halt fifty yards to the north and pointed at the ground.

Waterlogged brush grew thickly, but at least it wasn't a bog. She dropped to her knees and yanked at the undergrowth. Magic would've been cleaner and a whole hell of a lot faster, but it would also mark their presence—if anyone was looking. Her trousers soaked through immediately. Angus came at it from the other side of a huge clump of gorse, working his way toward her. A square of muddy earth studded with rocks came into view as they dug. If a gateway lay beneath, it hadn't been used in centuries.

Angus grabbed a large, flat rock and scraped dirt aside. A few inches down, the rock pinged against wood with a hollow *thunk*. He raised his gaze and jerked his chin at the hole in the ground. *"Now can we use magic?"*

She got a rock of her own and bent her back to help him. *"Not until we see the whole door. Mayhap 'twill be so rotten with mold, damp, and age, we willna need anything beyond rocks or my bow."*

"A girl can dream." He scraped harder.

Arianrhod rocked back on her heels and surveyed the door they'd exposed. Six feet by two feet, it was solidly built—or had been at one time. Wooden planks set into a rusted metal frame were recessed deep into the muddy soil. The entrance appeared so unused, she wondered if it led to anything beyond a dead end.

Strident bugling announced dragons returning. It sounded like the same pair she'd heard earlier, which suggested Malik and Preki returning to Rhukon's manor house. If luck was with her, the dragons would shift back into their mage forms. She drew the weave of her magic more tightly around them and stifled their presence down to nothing more than a whisper in the wet vegetation.

Rhukon was a dandy and an ass. Connor an inconvenience. But that was if she faced them as men. Facing them as dragons cast things in a much more perilous light—particularly for Angus. It disturbed her that he'd refused outright when she mapped out parameters and told him he'd need to leave if things got dicey. Being brave was one thing. Being foolhardy, quite another.

"I'm not leaving."

She snapped her head up and felt the heat of his gaze drill into her. *"Get out of my head."* She started to redirect her magic, but decided it wasn't a good idea.

A smug expression carved his features into self-assured lines. *"You can't have it both ways. Either you use your power to guard us from above, or you use it to keep me out."* He tilted his head. *"What's that?"*

She focused her hearing, augmenting it with what little power wasn't keeping them shielded. Dragon chatter gave way to the deep hum of men's voices, followed by a muted, clanging *thunk* as a door swung open and shut.

Angus leaned close. *"The dragons are men again."*

"Aye. We must get inside afore they harm Eletea." She eyed the gateway in the ground and decided to take a chance. A single blast of magic reduced the rusty hasps to smoking holes.

Angus surged forward and yanked hard. The door didn't budge because some of it was still submerged. He focused a stream of white light that washed over the door. Clods of muddy dirt flew everywhere. She ducked. Even so, one barely missed her head.

"Hold." She laid a hand over his and waited, barely breathing. Time slid past. One minute. Two. If Rhukon or Connor had felt a disturbance, they'd be out here by now, or at least headed their way.

He raised his brows in an unspoken question. At her nod, he pulled the door up and to the side.

She stared downward into darkness and summoned her mage light. It illuminated a set of rotting, wooden steps, so narrow negotiating them would be a neat trick.

"I'll go first." Angus swung his body into the hole. *"I'll let you know when I'm at the bottom, and you can come ahead. That way I can catch you if you fall."*

Part of her bristled at being ordered about, another part craved being coddled and cared for. She didn't want to sort through any of it, so she watched him disappear into the dank-smelling earth. At least it was a clean odor. This part of the underground tunnel system hadn't been used to sequester bodies—or for anything equally grisly.

"Now," rang in her head. She backed down steps more like a ladder than a staircase, ready for anything.

Angus spanned her waist with his strong hands and lowered her the last few feet. She kept her light low and gazed at rounded walls not quite tall enough for her to stand upright. Water ran down the walls, coming almost to her ankles. A phalanx of red eyes stared at her. Rats. High-pitched, nervous chittering filled the space, echoing off the walls.

"Friends," Angus suggested silkily.

The tenor of the rodents' vocalizations shifted from frantic to a normal cadence.

Arianrhod nodded briskly. *"Good. Now if we can just keep the bats from leaving, we'll be golden."*

"Soothing them was the first thing I did, even before I called you."

Pleased he'd thought of it, she plodded through standing water toward the manor house. Eventually, they'd hit the foundation, sunk deep into the earth. There'd likely be another gateway there, but not always. Side tunnels branched off from time to time. If she wasn't certain, she let Angus make the call. He was the one with the link to the dragon.

"Does she know we're coming?" Arianrhod asked.

"Nay."

"Are ye certain? Ye've been following her energy ever since we arrived. Surely she felt the twang when ye sighted her."

He shrugged and gestured for them to keep moving.

Arianrhod shrouded them with invisibility. Things were going along too well, and the deeper they got into the passageway, the edgier she became. Rhukon wasn't stupid. That was Connor's purview. He had to realize they were beneath his house. If the situation were reversed, she'd know.

Angus ground to a halt and pointed ahead of him at the rough stones of the manor house's foundation. They'd fallen in one spot and made a hell of a mess. There'd once been a door, but it was twisted almost beyond recognition by rock fall. Blasting their way through with magic was child's play, but they couldn't risk it. Not this close to the house.

Drawing himself up to his full height, Angus extended his hands. Before he could loosen anything that would give their presence away, she grabbed his wrist.

"Ye canna—"

He drew her hand to his mouth, planting a kiss on her mud-caked flesh. *"Relax. I hold different magics. It's why I'm so valuable to Arawn and the others."*

"What other magics?" She snatched her hand back from the wonderful warmth of his lips tickling it.

"I can blend my gift with the Earth. No one will sense a thing. I wasn't certain while we were still outside, but down here with earth all about us, I'm confident I won't give us away."

She nodded and stood back, giving him space to work. As she did, an odd feeling fluttered in her chest. She never gave the upper hand away, but she trusted the man by her side. Trusted him to take care of them. To do the right thing. It was such a revelation, she could barely keep her mouth from gaping open.

The fetid air in the tunnel thickened with a scent redolent of the salt tang of the sea mingled with the lush pine forest they'd left above. Angus drew a slender dirk from a thigh sheath. She remembered it clattering to the floor when they were pulling their clothes off, so anxious to get to one another's bodies, nothing else mattered.

A low hum reached her ears, and he drew the dirk along the tips of the fingers of his left hand. Once blood flowed, he scattered it on the tumble of rocks and earth that overflowed the space where the gateway had once been.

Between the scent and the song, Arianrhod felt herself drawn into Angus's magic. It was different from anything she'd ever felt before. Deep magic, hinting of the earliest mysteries. Colors shimmered around him as his blood sang to the stones. It grew warm in the tunnel, a deceptive warmth that could lure the unsuspecting to their deaths—if they didn't sense the steel beneath it.

Rocks are the bones of the earth.

Where had she heard that? She tried, but couldn't remember. Angus was of the earth, just like the stones shifting at his command.

Of the earth, yet not. It was why he could breach the time-travel portals. They were barred to mortals, yet not to him. Nessa and Cathbad. What had the combination spawned? Could he possibly be Conchobar, reborn through some shadowy mechanism?

The more she thought about it, the surer she was Arawn was behind Angus's appearance in modern time. Ceridwen and Gwydion may have been in on the plan, but the god of the dead could resurrect whomever he needed to do his bidding.

The sound of rocks grinding against one another quieted, and the temperature fell so quickly, she drew her leathers closer to her body. Angus's eyes glittered with the power he'd channeled, but the dirk wasn't in his hand any longer, nor did he have visible cuts on his fingertips.

He swept an arm toward the hole he'd made, and she stepped through. She had questions. Lots of them. She wanted to dissect his power. Understand its roots, but danger lay ahead. She felt a tightening in her belly that never presaged anything good.

Arianrhod turned to Angus and held up a hand. Not wanting to draw her own power so close to Rhukon and Connor, she mouthed, "Eletea?"

Angus pointed and held up five fingers followed by a circle. Fifty paces. That close. She shrugged her bow off her shoulder and nocked an arrow. Brigid had gifted her the golden arrows. Their magic meant she never missed.

Footsteps pounded down an unseen corridor. They'd left the realm of standing water on the far side of the manor house foundations. She'd stood ankle deep in it so long, she didn't notice the hard, dirt floor until the noise alerted her.

Angus gripped her shoulder and mouthed, "Wait."

She extinguished her mage light, expecting total darkness, but Angus glowed. Nothing to draw attention to them, but a soft white nimbus surrounded him.

"Still here, I see." A rough, male voice exclaimed.

"And where would I have gone with iron about my neck?" Multi-toned, accented words identified the speaker as Eletea. Dragon vocal chords gave them the ability to mimic any creature.

"Och, ye've been dreaming about having the both of us," a second male voice chortled. "Admit it, wench."

"I've always fancied lying with a dragon," the first voice said, his words such a seduction charade, Arianrhod nearly choked on indignation.

Light flared in the tunnel ahead of them. Dragon's fire.

Good for you! Arianrhod stabbed the air with a fist.

"That will never happen," Eletea announced. "You can kill me, but I'll take you out if you rape me. Besides..." Cunning entered her tones. "You'd end up dickless. Wouldn't that be special?"

"Absurd," the second man scoffed.

His voice was higher. Arianrhod was almost certain it was Connor.

"Want to find out?" The dragon challenged. "I have scales in the most unusual places. Sharp scales."

"Why hasn't your race died out?" Rhukon snarled.

"I can sheath them—if I choose. For you," Eletea paused, "I'd like nothing better than to castrate you, you sorry sack of shit."

"Enough!" Rhukon roared.

"Told you this was a waste of time," Connor cut in.

"Ye can jolly well shut your hole too," Rhukon countered.

Angus made come along gestures with one hand, but she sidled close and held onto his shoulder. Rhukon and Connor were deep enough into things with the dragon that Arianrhod risked a low whisper into his ear.

"We canna kill them. The dragon shifter bond made them immortal."

"We can injure them, so they'll take time to heal," Angus countered quietly. "What choice do we have?"

Ye could leave and let me battle alone. Immortal versus immortal.

He'd already refused that strategy, so she muttered, "I'll shoot Rhukon. Ye take Connor. Once we disable them, we'll still have to break Eletea's bonds and get out."

He winked broadly. "One thing at a time. We might not be able to kill them, but we can make them wish they were dead."

"What's that?" Rhukon's voice was sharp.

Damn it! He'd heard them.

"Now!" she screeched and raced down the tunnel, bow at the ready. She rounded a tight corner, and light spilled from a chamber ahead. Presumably the one where Eletea was held prisoner.

Arianrhod drew back her bow. She took aim and let the arrow fly as soon as Rhukon came into view. Long dark hair curled onto his shoulders, and fire flashed from his dark eyes. Steam rolled from his mouth. Malik's way of expressing his displeasure.

Before Rhukon could shift—since Malik obviously wanted out— she loosed a second arrow and watched in horrified fascination as it tracked an arc around the dragon shifter and lodged next to her first arrow in a wall behind him.

Apparently *never miss* didn't apply if she aimed for something immortal.

"What's your next trick, bitch?" Rhukon spat on the floor. His form flickered, illuminated from within, caught up in the change to dragon.

Angus threw himself at Connor, bearing the other man to the ground with his heavier weight. The same fey light flared around Connor, but Angus pulled his dirk and pinned the other man to the earth by driving it through his shoulder.

Connor writhed, screaming. Fire flashed from his mouth, followed by smoke and steam.

"Nice try." Angus drew his lips back into a snarl that bared his teeth. "No shifting for you. Not so long as you're locked to earth magic."

"Virgin huntress!" Eletea shouted. "Shoot my shackles. Hurry before Malik is fully present."

Arianrhod stared at the dragon. Holes had been drilled in her leathery copper-gold wings. Metal links ran through them into bolts fastened to the walls. "I could injure you."

"Doesn't matter." The elegance fled from Eletea's speech. "Just do it. Now."

Arianrhod didn't waste time worrying if the magic that subverted her last arrow would have the same effect on this one. Not much she could do about it if it did. She sighted and let a golden arrow fly straight at one of the shackles holding the dragon in place. A shower of sparks erupted as the arrow burrowed through an iron manacle.

With a high-pitched shriek of pain, Eletea wrenched one wing free. Blood flowed from the rent in it. "The other." She focused dark eyes with golden centers on Arianrhod, urging her to action.

A glance at a partially-shifted Rhukon told her she was running out of time. She loosed another arrow. For a moment, it looked as if it would pin the dragon more firmly to the wall behind her, but Arianrhod heaved magic after the arrow, and the shackle broke into pieces and clattered to the floor.

Eletea yanked her other wing free just as Malik lumbered around to face her, fire spewing from his mouth. The smaller dragon had a clear advantage because she could maneuver in what was a tight fit for Malik, who outweighed her by a good five hundred pounds.

Blood flowed down Eletea's wings in dark rivulets that dripped onto the packed earth floor, but she ignored her wounds. Fire flashed from her mouth, and she raised her red tipped talons to fighting stance. "What?" she demanded. "Will we burn the world around us to a cinder?"

"Ye're still under my command." Malik scored the walls with fire.

"In your dreams. Soon no one will be under your command. Once the others find out what you've done, you'll be banished from Fire Mountain."

"Ye just gave me a most excellent reason to make certain they never do. Ye're far from immortal, little dragon. Ye're barely past your first century. Ye have no hope of—"

Compulsion cloaked his words like thick honey, but Eletea appeared immune. Arianrhod smiled grimly when the young dragon rolled her shoulders with a clattering of scales and spat, "Give it up. Those old tricks won't work on me."

Magic flared around Angus as he built something—no doubt a fireproof shield—about himself and Connor. Cursing the half of her hair she hadn't bothered to braid, Arianrhod did the best she could to bundle the floor-length strands and tuck them beneath her top as she summoned a ward.

"I told you not to leave her alone," another dragon's voice—likely Danne, since he was the only one not accounted for—sounded from the far end of the cavern. He trotted into view, surprisingly agile for his size as he pushed past Malik's bulk. His scales were the same rich coppery-gold as Eletea's, but where her eyes were dark with lighter centers, his were pure gold from edge to edge.

"Why, Danne?" Eletea swung to face her egg-mate. "At least tell me why, so I'm not ashamed to call you brother."

"I might ask you the same thing." Fire forked from his mouth, but it bounced off Eletea. Dragons were impervious to the stuff. They'd been forged in it. "You killed my beloved. My mate."

Eletea shook her head. Smoke and fire-tinged spittle flew from her mouth. "You can't have a romance with your shifter bond mate. That's just wrong. No one does things that way."

"That doesn't make it immoral, only different," he replied in a wheedling, whiny tone.

"Shut up!" Malik roared. "Not the time for tea, crumpets, and talk."

"You broke our laws by bringing me here against my will." Eletea drew herself tall and faced Malik. "At the very least, you should be stripped of the bond with your human for that. Connor too."

"You broke them first by killing Mitha," Danne hissed.

"I didn't break anything." Eletea punctuated her words with a high bugle. "She was wicked. We kill evil."

Arianrhod caught movement out of the corner of her eye. She spun but was a hair too late. Malik scooped her off the ground with a taloned foreleg and held her tight against his black-scaled chest.

"Ye forget yourself." She writhed, but his grip tightened. She kicked his chest, but she may as well have kicked a boulder.

"Let her go!" Angus leapt to his feet, blade in one hand and power blazing from him so brightly he rivaled the dragons.

Danne focused flame on Angus's blade. It turned red hot, but he kept hold of it. When Arianrhod looked through her third eye, she saw cooling magic flow upward from the Earth. It shrouded Angus, protecting him from dragonfire.

Connor thrashed weakly on the ground. Angus barked a command, and the knife pinning him began to glow with a blue-white light. "Let her go," he repeated.

"Or?" Malik favored him with a toothy grin that displayed double rows of razor sharp teeth.

Angus squared his shoulders. "Or I won't rest until you're banished by your people. I might not manage to do away with you today, but I'll make it my life's mission to destroy you."

Arianrhod wanted to tell him to leave. Despite Malik's threats, the dragon couldn't harm her.

"Oh, but you're wrong." Malik swung her so she faced one of his whirling eyes. "Wipe that shocked look off your face. Your mind is like an open book to me. I can force you so far into the *Dreaming*, you'll never find your way back."

"Try it." She bridled, furious with the dragon, but even angrier with herself for allowing him to capture her.

"Is that true?" Angus asked.

"Nay. Aye. Maybe." She sputtered. "Legends suggest such a thing, yet 'tis never happened."

"Let's test it, Celt." Malik's voice radiated menace, the different tones clanging against one another discordantly.

Eletea planted herself squarely in front of Malik. "Your quarrel is with me. Let her go, and we can settle things the dragon way."

"Aye, I'd welcome a fight to the death with you...egg-mate." Danne hissed steam.

"Danne. Och, Danne. What the hell happened to you?" Eletea's voice held sadness and resignation.

"Save your pity." Malik tossed his head and focused on Danne. "Ye're not fighting anyone."

"Why the fuck not?" Danne blurted, fury lining his words. "We have an opportunity to avenge Mitha—"

"I'm not telling you to shut up again." Malik sneered. "She never cared about you. You were a means to an end for her. The only dragon stupid enough to manipulate. If I let the two of you"—he swung a wingtip to encompass Eletea and Danne—"have a go at each other, she'd win."

"You bastard!" Danne rushed Malik in a bevy of flame. "Mitha was mine. Mine. You have no right—"

Arianrhod waited until Malik's focus shifted to the dragon charging him. She wouldn't get a second chance to free herself, so she took her time. When she felt the talons gripping her middle like hedge shears loosen ever so slightly, she pulled an arrow from the quiver still across her back and drove it into Malik's eye in one fluid motion. The arrow developed its own momentum, so she didn't need brute strength.

Outraged dragon shrieks deafened her, and she kicked and

punched in an effort to escape his grasp. Angus's power pounded into her head, and she knew what to do. Weaving his magic with her own, she grasped the end of the arrow protruding from Malik's eye and sent a jolt of destruction into his brain.

The dragon let go of her so fast she fell like a stone, pulling magic like a mad thing to soften her fall.

"Got you." Angus closed his arms around her, steadying her before he let go.

Arianrhod blinked back tears from the smoke-filled room. Dragons trumpeted all around her, and everything that could burn in the chamber was on fire.

"Eletea!" Angus bellowed

"Here." The dragon's high, sweet voice sounded behind them.

"We're leaving," Angus told her.

"But I can't. I must kill—"

Arianrhod made her way through the smoke and cinder-filled air, batting out small fires that burned holes in her leather clothing. She almost ran into the dragon before she saw her. Eletea and Danne were locked in combat shooting fire into each other's faces. Blood ran from multiple wounds on both dragons.

Eletea cried as she fought, and a pile of gemstones formed around her feet from her tears. Arianrhod's heart clenched for the young dragon. She loved Danne. He was still her brother, but she recognized her duty to wipe out evil.

A partially blinded Malik blundered from one side of the underground chamber to another, hitting walls and screeching his pain. Connor was presumably still locked to the earth by Angus's magic.

"Stand back," Arianrhod roared. She nocked an arrow and sent it flying into Danne's open mouth. Dragons had a few weak spots. The arrow would penetrate the back of his throat and impale his brainstem. It wouldn't be a quick death, but he would die.

Danne bellowed as the arrow hit home, grappling at it with his talons as he tried to pull it free. Arianrhod tossed her head back, nostrils flaring. She still didn't understand how Rhukon had subverted her first two arrows, but she was confident Danne wouldn't be able to undo her marksmanship. His cries escalated before he slumped to the ground, still trying to work the arrow loose.

"We're done here," she told Eletea.

"Hurry," Angus exhorted. "Malik pulled your arrow out, and he's healing his wound."

"Fuck dragon shifter immortality," she muttered and drew magic to vault to Eletea's back.

After an outraged squawk, the dragon ran full speed for the far end of the chamber, pushing past Malik and Connor's prone form. Angus dragged his knife from Connor's shoulder and vaulted to the dragon's back behind her.

Once she realized they were together, Arianrhod shoved power into a working that would not only take them outside, but far from Rhukon's manor house.

They emerged into a full-fledged lightning storm with the sky cut by jagged bolts of electricity. Arianrhod leaned back into Angus's warmth. Somehow, they'd not only found Eletea, but saved her life.

"Get off my back," the dragon snapped through sobs. "No one rides me without my permission. No one."

Angus wrapped his arms around Arianrhod and used magic to cushion their descent. Once she was on her feet with rain pounding on her head, Arianrhod turned to the dragon. "Ye might offer us a spot of thanks," she suggested dryly. "Ye werena in a verra good position when we found you."

"Later," Angus muttered. "Let's get the lot of us back to Fire Mountain. Then we can dissect this all we want."

"Surely Rhukon and Connor wouldna be so stupid as to come after us," Arianrhod protested. "Both of them are wounded."

"The main thing wounded about Malik is his pride," Eletea spoke up. "I agree with the Seer. We must leave. I'll find my own way.

Here's yours." She sent a blast of dragon magic into the midst of the thunderstorm, and the outline of a time-travel shaft opened in the murk.

Arianrhod opened her mouth to say they'd finish this on Fire Mountain, but the dragon was gone, vanished into the teeth of the storm.

Angus gripped her arm and dragged her forward. "The dragon gave us a gift. I say we take it."

She was barely settled in the undulating tunnel when she heard the enraged blare of dragons on the hunt.

Angus barked a word, and the portal sealed them in. Arianrhod layered spells atop his to keep Malik and Preki, Connor's dragon, from following them into the shaft. Nothing would preclude the two showing up at Fire Mountain, but she didn't believe they'd be that rash. The other dragons would crucify them once they discovered what they'd done.

"Even I didn't think they'd be that close on our heels." Angus shook his head. "Was Rhukon always this vindictive?"

She curved her mouth into a grimace. "Aye, that and more. I always believed he courted the dragon shifter bond to ensure his survival. That one made enemies everyway he turned."

"I can see why." Angus glanced at a node as it sped past. "Fire Mountain, then where?"

"Let's get through this next confrontation with the dragons first." She was hedging, but she couldn't plan any sort of future that included Angus. It wasn't possible, no matter how much she might want to.

Arianrhod settled her body into a more comfortable position. So long as she had the time, she pulled her long, tangled hair from beneath her top and dragged her fingers through it. When most of the snarls had given way, she hastily created two more braids, securing them with pieces of leather drawn from her many pockets.

"You're quiet," Angus observed.

"Aye." She tilted her head and gazed into his marvelous eyes.

"Your magic is impressive. I've never seen the like. What do ye know of it?"

"Not much. I have strong affinity for earth and water. They protect me, and they heed my commands."

An idea formed. Before her own needs got the better of her, she said, "Would ye like me to help you return to your own time?"

He drew his brows together. "If you—or anyone—had asked me that before I met you, I'd have jumped on it."

Her heart fluttered in her chest, and a warm, buttery feeling spread through her. "And now?"

He grasped one of her hands. "Are you offering to come with me or merely open a gateway for me to travel through?"

She tried to say she'd just be doing some spadework to figure out where he belonged and help him get there, once she homed in on it, but the words curdled on her tongue. She didn't want to leave him anymore than he wanted to leave her. After a long silence, she finally admitted, "I doona know. Ye weaken my resolve."

The crooked smile she loved crossed his face. "If you're coming with me, of course I'd like to see where I came from. If not, I prefer to remain where you are."

Alarm bells rang so loud they deafened her, and she pulled her hand away. "It doesna matter what ye want, or what I want. We canna be together even long enough to decide if what flows between us is real."

"Why not? If it's just that virgin huntress thing—"

She held up a hand, and the rest of his words died when he looked at her. "'Tis who I am. I canna be aught but that. 'Twasn't as if I had a choice. Danu did the choosing. She assigned us roles. 'Tisn't like a factory job where I can turn in my keys and say *I quit.*"

"Why not?" he persisted and captured her hand again. "How many thousands of years do you owe them? Besides," he forged ahead, "it's not as if you have to hang up your sigil and your bow. You could—"

"It doesna work that way." She spoke over him, desperate to

drown out the longing spilling from her. "What if Arawn said he dinna wish to shepherd the dead anymore? Or if Ceridwen upended her cauldron, and the world grated to a halt?"

He stroked the back of her hand with his thumb. Shivers of wanting him cascaded through her, but she couldn't summon the strength to pull away from his touch.

"They're not the same." His deep voice rumbled, echoing slightly in their enclosed space. "And you know it. Your primary role in the Pantheon doesn't have much to do with enforced virginity. You're living a lie. The dragons know. I heard the undertone in their voices."

Old bitterness soured her stomach. He'd just voiced what had grated forever. Her role as moon-mother goddess was critical. The tides depended on her, but no one ever paid any attention to *that* part of things. No, it was her virgin huntress label that followed her everywhere. She examined a node. They'd be at their destination soon.

"We'll talk more of this later." She moved her hand from beneath his. "As I see things, we're back where we started with the dragons. We have yet to find a dragon who can speak for Eletea. That was our task. To clear her culpability in Mitha's death."

"Surely the dragons will be so grateful for her return, they'll dredge up a First Born."

"Not necessarily." She snorted. "We'll be lucky to get a thank you from them. Ye saw how the one we rescued ordered us from her back the moment we were clear of Rhukon's manor. Eletea's young, but her arrogance and sense of entitlement will grow with her."

"She was frightened when I first met her," Angus argued. "Worried she'd done wrong."

"Aye, and she cried when she took her egg-mate on in combat, yet she was sure enough of herself to not let her feelings for Danne get in her way."

"What are you suggesting?" Angus sounded tired.

She didn't blame him. Dragons lived by themselves for the best of reasons. Only other dragons could stand them. She'd never understood the lure of the dragon shifter bond. From where she stood, the only benefit was immortality.

Maybe I never met the right dragon…

Keene flitted through her memory. Truth followed. She'd been a diversion for him. Something different. He'd never cared about her, or he'd have hunted her down. As it was, he hadn't even been at Fire Mountain many of the times she'd gone looking for him.

"Ari?" Angus's voice was gentle. "We'll be there in just a few minutes."

"We'll round up that green who sent us after Eletea, tell her we did our part, and ask her to assure us the dragons will take care of determining Eletea's guilt or innocence in Mitha's death."

She dusted her hands together. "They willna be able to tell us no because we just did their bidding and returned one of their own."

"Just like that." He narrowed his eyes.

"Aye, just like that, but then we'll have to wait for their pronouncement, so we can ferry it back to the Celtic Council."

"Not necessarily. I can still dream the truth. I have more than enough information to work with if I summon a vision."

He checked a node, chanted low, and the shaft shuddered to a stop. One of the walls gaped open, and the time-travel tunnel tossed them out at the edge of a caldera spitting magma. Angus drew her back from the verge of the fiery pit. He glanced around and pointed. "We have quite a way to walk. We may as well get going."

She jutted her chin skyward at a dragon winging its way toward them. "It won't take all that long. Eletea must've told her kin we'd be right behind her. They were waiting for us."

CHAPTER 9

*A*ngus nodded at the red dragon who dropped like a stone, so close to them he had to fight an urge to step out of its way. It was an old game. The dragon equivalent of chicken to see who blinked first.

The dragon nodded back, approval mirrored in its whirling blue eyes. "Onto my back. Both of you."

Angus tossed magic over Arianrhod and boosted them onto the dragon. Arianrhod grasped the horns that grew from the base of the dragon's neck. Angus wrapped his arms around her, enjoying the press of her body against his chest. The dragon spread its wings and was airborne so fast the wind rush nearly unsettled him from his perch.

Fire Mountain spread beneath them in all its harsh, volcanic glory. He placed his mouth near her ear. "Do you have any idea when this world was formed?"

She shook her head. "'Tis always been here. Dragons are older than any of us."

"Do you suppose it's the original world? The one all the rest of them came from?"

She leaned into him and turned her head so her cheek was

against his. "I doona think so. The dragons seem anxious to have us front and center. Figuring out why is more important than a digression into history."

Angus thought about it. They'd left Fire Mountain in the midst of chaos to hunt down Eletea. If he knew anything about dragons, they liked to keep their dirty laundry under wraps. "I suspect they want to send us back to your kin with a carefully scripted message."

Her body shook with laughter that was torn away by the wind. "Now ye mention it, they'll likely want us to keep quiet about everything else."

"What's so funny, *virgin* huntress?" The dragon turned its head to stare back at them.

"She's just relieved we escaped Rhukon. So long as you feel like chatting, was Fire Mountain the first world?" Angus wanted to divert the dragon from heckling Arianrhod, and he was genuinely curious about the history of Fire Mountain.

"Of course this was the first world," the dragon huffed. It turned so it faced the way they traveled, but its next words were quite clear. "We're the first race, so naturally our world was formed from the ether before any others." It paused for a beat. "Our biggest mistake in all those years was that infernal dragon shifter bond."

"Most of the mages have been assets," Arianrhod pointed out.

"But the ones that turned rogue poisoned the well," the dragon replied. "Hang on. We're almost there."

It turned out to be good advice, since the dragon's bulk fell out of the air. Angus was reasonably confident they wouldn't crash. Dragons weren't into self-destruction, but the transition from air to ground took nerves of steel. Multi-tonal dragon laughter rang out as the creature spread its wings at what felt like the last possible moment, and they floated gently to cracked red dirt, studded with pumice and obsidian.

Angus summoned magic to move them to the ground, but Arianrhod beat him to it. "My turn." She smiled brightly once they were off the dragon's back.

He turned to thank the dragon, but its wings were already flapping, and it was gone before he could do more than shout, "Appreciate the ride," after it.

"Doesna bode well," Arianrhod muttered as she turned in a full circle, surveying where they were.

Angus recognized landmarks, though they were subtle on this world where everything looked much the same. "That way." He pointed. "Their council cave is just over that rise."

She began walking and he followed, enjoying watching the swing of her hips as she made her way over uneven terrain. Her bow and quiver bounced against her body, and four braids fell down her back, reaching almost to her knees. His body responded to her nearness at a bone-deep level. He'd never wanted a woman as much as he wanted Arianrhod.

She wanted him too—he felt her desire and her ambivalence—but she had everything to lose by joining her star to his. At least that was the way she saw things. He'd pushed earlier, trying to argue her away from her position, but he'd backed off. Maybe if he had an established spot anywhere, he'd cling to it with her tenacity. Recognition slapped him that she'd lived a lie so long, it had become second nature. She wasn't adverse to having sex—hell, maybe the other Celts even knew about her fall from grace—but to proclaim it openly challenged her spot in the Pantheon.

It's like me and Arawn both pretending he'd tell me about my origins. He knew he'd never do that, and I eventually figured it out, but neither of us ever voiced our knowledge. If we had, it would've changed our relationship. Made it impossible for me to pretend I was a free agent.

I'm not. Never have been.

The next question, when it came, shook him. *What the fuck am I going to do about it?*

Arianrhod stopped fifty paces from the mound leading into the council cave and turned to face him. "Ye're troubled. What are ye thinking about?"

"Why not just bore into my head?" He sounded surly, but couldn't help it.

"Because I respect you more than that." She leveled her gaze at him. "No matter how things turn out between us, doona doubt that I care for you."

He unclenched his jaw. No reason to be angry with her. Both of them were caught up in something bigger than they were. "We can talk after we get through whatever the dragons have in store for us."

"Mayhap we could have that conversation while we travel to search out your origins."

Hope slammed into his gut so hard he had to hold himself back from drawing her into his arms. "You'll come with me."

"Aye." Her golden and silver eyes twinkled. "We owe one another that much, and 'twill offer an opportunity to sort things out." She held up a hand. "Doona hope for too much from me. What ye want shines from you like a beacon, and it may well be more than I can give."

"But you want the same thing."

A pinched look formed around her eyes. "I want many things. Contradictory things. I've lived with compromise so long, 'tis become like a contrary twin." She shook her head before turning toward the council cave.

He understood she'd said all she was going to and trotted to her side. Whatever the dragons had in mind, they'd face it together. He walked behind her until they ducked inside the opening into the mound. The outer chamber where he'd first met Arianrhod was deserted. Unlike their last visit that had been punctuated by dragon screams and smoke-filled air, the outer cave was absolutely silent.

"So far so good," he muttered.

"Aye." She quirked a brow. "At least the natives doona appear to be restless."

"This way." Angus set a brisk pace for where the Dragon Council set up shop. "Be warned, it gets even warmer as we move down."

After several twists and turns in long tunnels excavated deep into the mountainside, the muted hum of dragons talking in their musical language reached his ears. It reminded him of the Selkies' tongue. He covered the last distance and walked into an enormous chamber with Arianrhod by his side. Pale green limestone lined the walls, and the ceiling arched so far above his head, he couldn't see it in the relative darkness broken only by glowing dragons. He looked about for Eletea. When he didn't see her, he hunted for her energy with magic.

Not here.

The green dragon who'd sent them to fetch her lumbered forward. "We sent her to her home cave here on Fire Mountain. She doesn't need to be party to our discussion."

Angus squared his shoulders. "It's not polite to help yourself to someone's thoughts."

The dragon shrugged, making her scales jangle against one another. "Your customs don't concern me."

"If ye've already dispatched Eletea," Arianrhod broke in, "what do ye need from us?"

"She told us you killed Danne." The green's eyes whirled faster.

"She spoke true." Arianrhod held her ground. "Danne would've done the same to me."

"Aye, but you're immortal, so it was scarcely a fair contest." The green took a step closer.

Power flared around Arianrhod, lighting a circle about her. She strode forward until she couldn't get any closer to the dragon and still look up at her. "I may be immortal, but he"—she jerked a thumb at Angus—"isna. Eletea was locked to a wall by shackles through her wings when we arrived. Had Angus not disabled Connor, we'd have had to face three dragons to do your bidding and free Eletea."

"Malik says you injured him." Another dragon, this one black, joined the green. Amber eyes skewered Arianrhod.

"How the hell would you know that?" Angus demanded. "He's not here. Or is he?"

"Dragons can communicate over space and time," Arianrhod

murmured and tilted her chin at a defiant angle. "Aye." She addressed the black. "I drove an arrow through his eye. He held me between two talons, suspended many feet above the ground. What? Am I prohibited from defending myself? Had I known that, I'd have refused to go after your missing dragon." She paused long enough to suck in a breath. "Dragons are forbidden from threatening the Celtic gods. If anyone broke the compact between us, 'twas him, not me."

"Is the only reason we're here to defend ourselves against your accusations?" Angus asked, battling incredulity.

"You killed a dragon," the green said. "Did you believe we'd ignore something so blatant as that?"

"If ye dinna like how we handled things, ye should've taken care of the matter yourself." Arianrhod crossed her arms beneath her breasts. "We're not the ones who allowed Danne to infiltrate your ranks and make off with Eletea."

"Oberon's balls!" Angus fumed, staring at the green and black dragons. "You're worse than the Celts. At least once they task me with something, they turn me loose to accomplish it in my own way."

"Enough!"

A golden dragon larger by half than the other two dragged its bulk from the shadowed gloom at the rear of the cave. Dragons continued to grow as years passed, so this one must be over two thousand years old.

"I am Eagon, head of this council." The gold inclined his head. "The others are understandably concerned about the death of one of our own. Dragons are hard to replace."

"So are Celtic gods." Arianrhod swung to face him.

"You're immortal."

She narrowed her eyes. "Aye, but it doesna mean I shall walk the earth forever. I can be forced into the *Dreaming* by misfortune—or choice. Malik reminded me of that. 'Tisn't so different from being dead."

"Not relevant." Smoke puffed from the gold dragon's mouth, and the low murmur of dragons conversing rose and fell around Angus. The dragon raised a taloned foreleg and flexed claws as golden as the rest of him. "You're still immortal."

Irritation rolled off Arianrhod, and the glow around her developed a reddish tinge. "What of Malik? Will he be punished? How about Connor?"

"Connor isn't part of this. He sat out the disagreement."

"Only because I disabled him," Angus cut in, sick of the dragons' arrogance. "What about Eletea? What can I report to Ceridwen? Have you had her read—or whatever it is you do—by a First Born?"

The gold exchanged a pointed glance with the green. "My but they ask a lot of questions."

"Answer the one about Eletea. Tell me how Malik will be censured, and then we'll be gone," Arianrhod retorted.

"My decision regarding Malik is this." The golden dragon eyed her so coldly, Angus wanted to strangle him. "He was given a choice regarding his bond with Rhukon, and he asked to maintain it."

"We saw no reason to deny him," the green cut in.

"No reason?" Angus stalked closer. "He and Connor teamed with Danne to kidnap Eletea."

"They say they didn't. That Danne acted independently."

Arianrhod rolled her eyes. "I thought the Celts were insufferable protecting their own, but they're pikers compared with dragons."

Steam poured from the golden dragon, and he opened his jaws to speak, but Arianrhod held up a hand. "I'm not finished. When ye," she swung her gaze to the green, "sent us after Eletea, ye said Danne drew power far beyond him. I believe your exact words were, 'this holds the stink of dragon shifter magic gone bad.'"

The green's scales rattled as she shook herself. "I overreacted."

Angus moved to Arianrhod's side. "We should leave."

"Not until I receive a satisfactory answer about Malik and Rhukon. And we canna leave until we know about Eletea."

"I can dream the truth of that," he reminded her.

"Aye, but ye canna forge a fitting punishment for Malik that way. Or can ye?" She shifted her focus from the dragons to him.

"I don't know," he said quietly. "My magic is still showing itself to me."

"The day you turn your power against a dragon will be the day we destroy you, Seer." The gold angled his head and hurled smoky flames at Angus. He jumped to one side, narrowly avoiding them.

"What about dragon shifters?" Arianrhod continued. "The dragon who brought us here seemed to think—"

"You overstep yourself, Celt," the gold broke in. "Dragons don't court intrusion from others into our business."

"We need to leave," Angus said again. "Let Ceridwen handle this."

"I can fight my own battles," Arianrhod retorted.

"Be satisfied we're allowing you to leave," the gold dragon said through a shower of fire. "The last one from your bloodline who killed a dragon wasn't so fortunate."

Angus dredged through his memory and couldn't come up with a single Celt who'd slain a dragon but kept his mouth shut. He'd take anything that got them out of this cave. He'd never looked at dragons in quite the light he saw them today. Alien creatures who interpreted the world far differently than humans. Dragons held one another to different standards that flexed depending on circumstance. No matter how long Arianrhod argued, it was clear the dragons wouldn't lift a claw against one of their own.

Arianrhod clanked her teeth together and dropped her arms to her sides. "Ceridwen and the rest of my kin will receive a full report."

Dragon laughter brayed, spraying Angus with bits of cinder and spittle. "You do that, *virgin huntress*."

Color splotched across Arianrhod's high cheekbones, and the glow around her made a full commitment to an angry red. "Why you pretentious, egotistical—"

"Enough." Angus grabbed her arm.

"I'll leave when I'm ready," she informed him. Fury blazed from her eyes.

The dragon's council cave grew indistinct. Angus hoped to hell the dragon was moving them outside and not to the bottom of a magma-infested caldera. A tight breath rattled from his lungs when the scorched heat of night on Fire Mountain closed about them. Twin moons transited the sky, glowing blood red. When he glanced around, they weren't anywhere close to the mound leading to the council chamber, but that was likely just as well.

"Those bastards." Arianrhod punched her fist into a nearby boulder, shrieked in pain, and punched the air.

"They did seem worse than usual," Angus agreed. "Not that I've had all that much experience with dragons."

"Nay." She stuck her wounded knuckles in her mouth for a moment. "They werena any different. Mayhap ones ye've seen afore were on their good behavior." She shook her head, and strands of hair escaped from her braids and fell across her face. "I canna believe they're not going to so much as censure Malik."

Angus thought about it. "I think I know why," he ventured.

She spun to face him. "Spit it out."

"Because of his bond to Rhukon."

"Ye'll have to say more than that."

"The dragons only control Malik's segment of the partnership. They have zip in the way of influence over Rhukon."

Her eyes widened in sudden understanding. "They're worried someone would call them to task if they severed the shifter bond, thus potentially harming Rhukon."

"Exactly." Angus nodded. "Same would hold true for Connor, sorry piece of shit that he is. What exactly happens to the mage side of things if that bond is separated?"

"Good question." She cast her gaze skyward and closed her teeth over her lower lip, thinking. "Obviously, they'd lose their immortality, but beyond that I believe they risk madness. Not having the dragon in their minds leaves such a void, they might not be able to move past it."

"Has it ever happened?"

She smiled grimly. "I have no idea."

"You're not done with this, are you?"

"Clever of you. Nay, I'm not, but I can put it on hold for a while. The Celtic Council's not much quicker than the dragon one at decision making."

The ground rumbled ominously beneath them. Angus snorted back laughter. "They seem to be encouraging us to leave."

"Ye think?"

Angus laughed outright. "Whenever you come up with a modern twist of phrase like that, I do a double take."

"Aye, well, 'twouldn't do for me to be stuck in the sixteen hundreds now would it? Or Roman times or even afore that."

"Nay." He mimicked her brogue. "'Twouldn't do at all. Where to?" He summoned magic to bring a time-travel shaft into being.

"The past." She grinned engagingly. "Where else would we find your roots?"

CHAPTER 10

"I want to stop before we get to whatever destination you have in mind." Angus caught Arianrhod's gaze and held it. They'd been quiet since entering the time shaft, each presumably lost in their own thoughts.

"Why?"

"We never ran down a First Born, so we need information about Eletea to report back to the Celtic Council."

She glanced at a node and quirked a brow. "How's twelve hundred?"

"It'll do as well as any other time. I need quiet, though, so let's try to avoid the middle of the Crusades."

"I'll do my best." Dry humor warmed her words, and the glow of the tunnel added bright highlights to her silver hair. "The worst of the fighting was over by then, so we should be safe enough."

Rumbling undulations in the living shaft around them signaled a stop was imminent. The wall across from Angus split, and he stood before extending a hand to help Arianrhod to her feet. They walked into a damp evergreen forest with water sheeting from the sky. It dripped from all the greenery, and standing water pooled around their feet. A crisp snap told him the time shaft had disappeared.

"Still in the U.K., I see." Angus chuckled.

"It could be the Pacific Northwest in the States," she retorted.

Angus shook his head. "Doesn't smell the same. Everything there is newer. Have you been here before?"

"Not this exact spot, but this time." She rolled her eyes. "Hell, I lived through it. We might find a stone hut to shelter in while ye enter a trance. How long will ye need?" Water ran off a leather hood she'd pulled over her hair and dripped from her body. Her leather garments that had begun to dry from their stint in Rhukon's time darkened again.

"Each trance is different, but not more than an hour." He cast an appraising glance her way. "If we're set upon, I won't be able to help. At least not for a while. It takes a few minutes once I return before things are normal again."

"Got it." Magic shimmered around her as she sent it spinning in a broad arc. "Good news. I know where we are. An extensive cave system isna far from here. That might work better than a hut where the owner could return at any time."

"More caves." He blew out a breath. "I had enough of them on Fire Mountain to last a while."

"We could set up camp beneath a tree." She shook her head, and droplets hit him in the face.

"I'll deal with my antipathy. A nice, dry cave would be perfect. Besides, I'll need a fire."

She set off, and he fell into step next to her. They made their way through tangled undergrowth that hid deep pools. After a quarter mile, his boots were soaked through.

"What else will you need?" she asked.

"Just fire—and my own blood."

"Ye used blood to clear debris from beneath Rhukon's manor house," she observed.

"Aye, that I did."

Interest flashed from her eyes, but she redirected her gaze to the ground after she stumbled over submerged roots. "Will ye say more about that?"

"I'd love to, but it's part of what's been hidden from me. I've discovered what I know—which isn't much—by experimenting." Misty air, pouring rain, and thick timber obscured his vision. When a vertical red earthen hillside reared before him, he stopped abruptly, not prepared for it. Heather and gorse grew in dense clumps a hundred feet above him, and thick vines snaked their way up the cliff.

The air around Arianrhod glistened as she summoned power. With a downward sweep of one arm, she cut through enough thorn-studded vegetation that a rough doorway came into view. "Come on." She crooked two fingers his way.

"Don't we want to patch things up out here? If anyone happens by, they'll know someone's within."

She disappeared through the opening, and he followed, grateful to get out of the rain. Arianrhod waited off to the side of a small round entry portal. Broken stones littered the floor where animals had kicked them getting into or out of the cavern. The ceiling was low enough, he couldn't stand upright.

"No one will wander by," she said.

"How can you know?" He placed his hands on his knees before shaking water off himself.

"Men used to be far more superstitious. This cave system was rumored to house restless spirits of the dead." Illumination flared as she called her mage light.

"Did shades really take up residence here?" Angus followed her into a long, low tunnel with water running down its sides. Moss grew in places, and the gleam of eyes reflected off Arianrhod's light. Rats, lots of them. With a cacophony of high-pitched squeals, they fled in the opposite direction.

"Does it matter?" She glanced over one shoulder.

He didn't answer, but reached outward with magic. No one had lived in this cave system but mice, rats, and bats for long years. People had lived here, though. He could still smell residue from fires. The corridor ended abruptly, and he found himself in an oblong space perhaps twenty paces across. At least the ceiling extended above his head, and he straightened to get the kinks out of his back.

This cavern was drier with different rock. Gray-green limestone walls arched around him. He called his own light into being and walked through the small space, locating a hearth at one end. Soot trailing up the wall indicated a natural draft mechanism. All he needed was something to burn. Everything was wet, but he could dry it with magic.

"Will this do?" Arianrhod gazed at him.

"Perfectly." He moved past her, intent on retrieving tinder from outside.

"Where are you going?"

He stopped and turned toward her. "I need fire. I told you that."

"Let's see if there's not something left in here. Give me a moment." She sprinted away from him down one of three corridors branching off the room they stood in.

"I'll look too," he called after her and picked a different passageway. This one opened into a much larger grotto that held stronger remnants of human scents. He cast his light around the space and frowned. Bones, presumably human from the look of them, lay scattered in one corner, but so did several piles of wood.

He picked his way around the bones, clearly the work of marauding animals, and gathered an armload of tinder—as much as he could carry. All he needed was to get a blaze going. His power would keep it burning until he was done, but it would be nice to warm the cave enough to dry their clothes. The smaller space where he intended to work should heat up nicely.

He met Arianrhod in the short tunnel leading back to the space they'd decided to use. She glanced at the wood in his arms. "Is there more back there?" At his nod, she worked her way around him and disappeared from sight.

By the time she returned, he had a blaze going in the hearth in the small grotto. She dumped an armload of wood over what he'd carried in. "Will this be enough?"

"Aye. You won't need to feed it once my magic takes over."

She nodded solemnly. "What will I have to do?"

"Keep watch." He stripped off his coat and hung it from a rock protruding from the wall above his fire.

"Is there a particular way to rouse you if it becomes necessary?" She hunkered in front of the fire and extended her hands.

"The Gaelic chant to raise the dead."

She laughed, and the clear, crystalline tones warmed him as much as the fire. "Ye're joking."

"Nay, I'm not."

He considered turning back his shirtsleeves, but decided to take the soaked woolen garment all the way off. He needed his blood to flow into the fire. Having a sodden shirtsleeve drop over his incisions would create problems he didn't need.

Arianrhod whistled appreciatively. "And are ye planning to remove aught else? Is sex part of the incantation?"

He wished it were. "Nay to both, lass."

"Lass is it? Ye're scarcely Scottish." Another warm chuckle.

"I don't know what I am." He drew the dirk from his waist sheath and went to her side, squatting next to her. "Once I begin, you mustn't disturb me unless we have to leave this place."

"I ken that well enough."

He brushed his lips across hers, lingering just long enough to bring all his senses to aching life. He wanted her, but he needed all his energies to call a specific trance state. When they came to him, they brought power. When he forced them, they drained him.

Angus straightened and walked to the fire, chanting low. When he was above the blaze, he made horizontal cuts in his forearms and held them over the fire until his blood dripped into the flames, making them shoot higher. He chanted more firmly, anchoring his blood to the fire, exhorting it to work for him. Earth and water bent to his command without his blood to bind them—though blood intensified his efforts. Fire required his blood, and air ignored him completely.

He slowed his breathing until it matched his blood. One breath, one drop. The edges of his vision hazed, and he dropped into the world of dreams holding an image of Eletea firmly in his mind.

The copper dragon came into view, cloudy at first, then clearer. She was in a familiar place, and then he recognized Loch Linnhe near Fort William. Another dragon shouted at her and spouted flame. She shouted back at the red dragon, clearly distressed. Tears gathered in her eyes, and gemstones flooded to the grassy vale beneath her feet.

Angus asked for more from whomever brought his vision states. What were Eletea and the other dragon saying? He could see them, but it was like watching a silent movie. Was the red dragon Cavet? They didn't seem much like lovers. He felt himself slipping from trance and forced himself to neutral ground. Emotional reactions might bring things to a crashing halt, and there were no guarantees he could resurrect his dream state.

Eletea's head drooped. She spread her wings and flew away still dropping gemstones. The red dragon tossed its head and flew in the other direction.

Angus forced himself to breathe evenly. He hated choice points in trance. He could follow one or the other, but not both. Sometimes he tossed the decision to the gods, but not today. Fueled by intuition, he followed the red dragon. On the far side of a band of cliffs, the red banked and landed. Another dragon lumbered from the mouth of a cave.

Angus peered hard. At first, he thought it was Eletea, which wasn't possible since she'd flown the other way. Then he recognized Danne, her egg-mate. A cold tongue of rage built in his belly, but he pushed it aside.

No emotion.

None.

Danne inclined his head at the other dragon, who lumbered to him. "I made her angry," the red announced, "but she won't stay gone long."

Thank the gods I can hear now.

Angus tilted his head, not wanting to miss anything.

"Doesn't matter. We don't need long," Danne replied. "Mitha has a friend who wishes to bond with you. We can formalize the shifter bonds in ten nights' time during the full moon."

"Once it's done, we'll both be immortal." The red, who had to be Cavet, opened his jaws in a parody of a smile.

"What are you going to do about Eletea?" Danne asked.

"Why do you care?"

Danne at least had the grace to look chagrined. "She's my egg-mate, and she loves you. Not only that, she loves the Highlands."

Cavet shrugged. "All women love me." He leaned close to the smaller dragon. "I have a plan. By the time I'm done, she'll be so busy explaining herself, she won't be a problem any longer."

"What do you have in mind?" Danne's question came slowly, almost as if he didn't want to know.

"I'll tell the Council she's been dabbling in witchcraft and had sex with a human. After that, I'll tell them I'm so distraught, I don't want her anywhere near the Highlands anymore."

Danne's golden eyes whirled faster. "Can't you just tell her you changed your mind? It's easier, cleaner—"

"Not nearly as much fun." Cavet spoke over him. "You should leave. If she catches you here, she'll ask a lot of questions."

"No, she won't, but I'll go." He spread his copper wings, but he must've summoned magic as well because he vanished moments after becoming airborne.

Fury burned through Angus. He forced it into submission. He had to see what happened next.

Sure enough Eletea winged into view a short time later and landed close to Cavet, who clumped toward her. "Darling," he crooned. "I'm so sorry. We shouldn't fight."

She tilted her snout skyward, scenting the air. "Someone was just here."

"Don't be ridiculous." Angus could see the edges of a believability spell woven into those three words. "Come hunt with me."

"We shouldn't remain here."

"But it's ever so much nicer than modern times where we have to hide from humans and drain our magic remaining invisible as we dodge airplanes, drones, and helicopters."

"If you wish to remain in the past, we must receive permission from the Council. You know the rules as well as me, Cavet."

"My little stickler. Very well. We can return. Would you prefer Fire Mountain or the Highlands two hundred years from now?"

Weariness flowed from Eletea in palpable waves, and Angus's heart went out to the dragon. She loved Cavet, and that love would spell problems for her. Big ones.

"Our own time," she said at last. "It's closer, and I'm tired."

The dragons shimmered before his eyes as the vision dissipated. He fell to his knees and sent magic to repair the wounds in his arms. Arianrhod came near; her scent surrounded him, and she wrapped him in an embrace from behind. He leaned into her as he secured his spirit inside his body. It ranged free while he was in trance, which was why it took time to recover.

"Here." She handed him a flask. "'Tis mead. I always carry some tucked into my quiver."

"Resourceful woman." He took the silvery flagon and drank deep, feeling the fragrant liquor revive him.

She drew him to a sit on the hearth in front of the fire. The stones were pleasantly warm. "Tell me," she said. "Everything."

She knit her brow into angry lines as the tale unfolded. "We must warn her," she said when he'd finished.

"I agree." He shook off the last of the malaise from his vision state. "It's curious. She didn't say anything about another dark mage being there when she lured Mitha off to kill her."

"Mayhap Danne changed his mind. Ye said he seemed mildly

upset by Cavet's cavalier treatment of his egg-mate." Arianrhod closed her teeth over her lower lip. "I'm almost sorry I did away with him."

"Don't be." Angus placed an arm around her shoulders and pulled her against him. "He could've stayed out of sight on the upper floors of Rhukon's manor or in the back of that huge room. He joined the fight of his own free will. For that matter, he could've freed Eletea while Rhukon and Connor were flying around outside in dragon form. He didn't."

Arianrhod leaned into him, and they passed her flask back and forth in silence until she said, "We doona know if Cavet met the other dark mage who offered to bond with him."

"True. We also have no idea what the Fire Mountain dragons have in mind for Eletea."

"Do ye suppose Cavet had an opportunity to spread lies about her? It might be why her kin whisked her off once we arrived."

"One of the problems with dream states," Angus spoke slowly, "is it's hard to place them in time."

"Mayhap not so hard." Arianrhod straightened and leaned toward the fire. "Danne said ten days until the full moon."

"We don't know which full moon, though."

"Let's presume 'tis the one that just passed two nights since."

Angus recreated when Eletea had come to him and worked forward from there. "If it is, that might mean Mitha never brought the other dark mage to the Highlands."

"Aye, but it doesna mean Cavet dinna seek her out himself after Mitha's death."

Angus narrowed his eyes. "I'll bet Rhukon and Connor have answers. Dark mages hold court with one another."

A menacing light shone from Arianrhod's features, turning her beauty into something harsh and terrible. "Mayhap we can pay them a visit on our way back. 'Twill give us ammunition for another visit to Fire Mountain."

"Why do we need ammunition?"

"They all but booted us out of there. They're furious with me because of Danne and Malik. Do ye believe they'll welcome us waltzing back into their home world without a good reason?"

"I assumed you'd tell Ceridwen what we found, and she'd take it from there."

"Aye, and she'd verra much like to, but I want to keep the Morrigan out of things." Arianrhod laid a hand on the side of his face and turned him to face her. "Nothing we canna handle ourselves."

Light blazed from her eyes and drew him in. He felt his body respond to her power. Desire for him spilled from her in shimmering, incandescent waves. He threaded his hands into her hair above and below her braids and held her head just gazing at her. She was so beautiful, breath clotted in his throat. Silvery brows cut across her high forehead like birds' wings. Well-formed cheekbones led to a perfect jaw. He traced the lines of her face with his fingertips before moving to her broad shoulders. Then lower, cupping her breasts through her soft leather top. Her nipples were already hard, and they grew even more rigid beneath his touch.

Her full lips parted in an inviting smile. "We have time. Not only that. So long as we've come this far, we'll hold to our plan to seek out Cathbad after we leave here. I took advantage of the span of minutes ye spent in trance and used your fire to locate him."

Angus barely heard her. The nearness of her body and her heady scent drove everything from his head but desire for the woman curved into his arms. Maybe because he'd done it before, the laces of her clothing yielded much faster this time.

CHAPTER 11

*L*ust was like a live thing clawing at her. Arianrhod wanted the man in her arms beyond wisdom. Beyond reason. To leave the warm, cozy grotto without making love was unthinkable, unbearable. When he pulled the laces of her top aside, she helped him slide it over her head. He wove his arms around her and drew her against him, skin to skin. Her arms found their way around him with a mind of their own. His naked chest felt magnificent next to her breasts, and she explored the rich muscles of his back with her palms and fingers.

He murmured low in Gaelic telling her she was beautiful, special, his. She thought she should draw back, be strong, be the virgin huntress of legend, but she wanted him more than an archaic title. He rained kisses on her hair, and when he cupped the side of her face in his hand and angled her head, she welcomed his mouth on hers.

His lips demanded everything of her. She met his challenge and opened her mouth to his questing tongue. She nipped and sucked his mouth, tongue, and lips while tightening her hold on his back. Muscles rippled under her fingers, so she dug her nails into the sheet of flesh undulating beneath her touch.

He groaned and held on tighter, clinging to her as if she were his salvation in a world racing out of control. She could relate, since she felt the same way. Their kiss developed its own rhythm and cadence, extending outside time. She'd never been so aware of her body. Of sparks of sensation cascading through her, igniting yet more sparks until she was on fire from head to toe. When she opened her eyes, light spilled from her and Angus, illuminating the grotto with magic.

He dragged his mouth from hers and moved it down her neck. She arched her back and buried her hands in his hair as he kissed and nipped her breasts. The pressure of his mouth licking, teasing, biting made her belly clench. When he moved a hand between her legs, an orgasm spooled from her, leaving her shaken and desperate for more.

She reached for his cock and realized they both still had not only their trousers, but their boots on. "Clothes," she mumbled and used his body as a ladder to reposition herself so she could unlace his boots.

"Are you always this practical?" He favored her with an impish grin, and her heart melted right along with the pool of heat between her legs.

"Aye, that would be me." She smiled back, and bent to his feet again.

A tug told her he was doing the same thing to her. Once he'd stripped off her boots and stockings, he closed his mouth over her big toe. A flare of excitement raced up her leg until it felt as if he were sucking on her nubbin. Slowly, almost lazily, he moved to the next toe and the one after that. Her back arched like a bow and she slotted fingers between her legs to bring the next climax to life. Sound filled the cave as she shrieked her delight.

Angus raised his head from her feet and slithered far enough up her body to undo her leather breeches. She helped him push them down her legs, followed by her smallclothes. "Only thing left," she said, her breath coming fast, "is your trousers."

"You just want to see me naked." He reached for the fastenings on his pants and slid out of them, moving the rest of the way up her body until he could gather her into his arms. The swell of his erection pressed into her belly, and she snaked a hand between them to curve her fingers around him.

Gods but he felt amazing in her hand. Cocks had always fascinated her, but his was vibrant, alive in a way she'd never encountered before. Suddenly, she couldn't wait another minute. "Now," she urged in a voice she barely recognized as her own.

"Aye, lass," was followed by a string of Gaelic endearments.

He knelt above her, and she wrapped her legs around his waist, opening herself for him. His whiskey-colored eyes never left her face as he lowered himself into her body. She was as keyed up as if her earlier orgasms hadn't happened, couldn't wait for him to move inside her. He supported himself on his arms, and she wrapped hers around his torso and tightened her muscles around his shaft.

A song filled her mind, heavy with longing. It gave her pause until she recognized his soul calling to hers. For the first time ever, she let her barriers fall, accepted him into all of her, not just her body, but her heart and mind. The song changed, charged with joy so poignant it moved her to tears. The light surrounding them crackled and flashed, mirroring the intensity of what flowed between them.

When he began moving in and out of her, she met his body with her own. They became elemental, timeless, as one climax kindled the next. He shuddered inside her, and then came again, as swept up in their passion as she was.

When he finally lowered himself atop her, gasping and panting, she heard yet a third note enter their shared song and understood. A child would grow within her after today's lovemaking—if she let it.

He held her against him, and the solid beat of his heart reverberated against her ear. "I love you," he said in Gaelic. "My world, my heart, even if we were to never see one another again, you've given me such a gift."

She rocked him against her. The moment was so perfect, words would come short of reflecting the emotion shooting through her.

"I hope you didn't mind the music," he said once their breathing quieted. "It rose through me, and I couldn't control it."

"Why would I mind?" She pushed away enough to look at him, to trace the lines of his face with her fingertips.

"I suspect the song is there because a Selkie taught me the link between music and loving."

Arianrhod smiled. "When next ye see her, thank her for me."

"If I see her, I'll do that." He kissed her forehead. "There'll never be another woman in my arms besides you, not after what we just shared."

His words brought the quick bite of tears behind her lids. She wished things were different, that she was just a woman, and he just another man, but she knew better. She wanted their time in this cave, locked out of time and memory, to last forever, but they had work to do. "I doona want to, but we should leave."

"I've been feeling guilty myself. Maybe we could skip Cathbad. I'm worried about Eletea. Now that I know who I'm looking for, I can always return later and find him on my own."

"Nay, we willna skip Cathbad. 'Tis but a short journey, and he at least holds answers to whether ye are his son, Conchobar, or a more distant relation."

She extricated herself from his embrace and reached for her discarded clothing, watching him from beneath lowered lids. What a beautiful man, not just his body, but his spirit shone so brightly, it nearly blinded her when she looked through her third eye. Their time together was clearly destined, but she needed to decide the child's fate and what she'd tell Angus. Afraid he might figure it out anyway, she buried the knowledge deep.

"You're quiet," Angus said in between getting his clothes on.

"I'm happy," she replied. "It's such a foreign feeling, I'm making certain I doona forget how it feels."

"Know what you mean." He strolled to where she'd left her bow and quiver, picked them up, and walked across the cave to hand them to her.

She tucked her empty flask inside the quiver and let him guide her to her feet. "Wonder if it's still raining."

"We'll find out soon enough." He ruffled her hair, and the two of them broke out laughing.

"Aye," she said between bursts of mirth. "There's so much joy, 'tis spilling out all over everything."

"Are you complaining?"

She shook her head and dove into his arms for another hug before she looped her bow and quiver over a shoulder. For the barest moment, she let herself long for a life with him, with their son, but reality intruded and she reined in her yearning.

'Tis so much more than I had afore I met him, I'll live each moment and treasure them. The future will be quick enough to assert itself.

ANGUS KEPT an arm firmly around her and led them back to the cave's entrance. Night had fallen, but it had stopped raining, and the almost full moon lit a sky scattered with thousands of shining stars.

"What a glorious night," she said and blew a kiss at the moon. Her moon.

"It's like it was designed for us." He felt light, buoyant, different. What he'd told her back in the cave was true. His life had changed in an elemental way when they made love. He couldn't go back, nor did he want to.

She cocked her head to one side and looked like a girl for a moment. "We could return to where we entered this time period, but magic is closer to the surface here. I'll bet we can summon the time shaft, and it'll come to us."

Angus believed they could do anything, but the words sounded hokier than hell, so he just nodded and lent a stream of magic to help. Now that the mystery of his origins was about to be laid bare, part of him wanted to surge forward; another part didn't want to know.

The air around them came alive with power, pulsing and glistening as a portal formed a few feet away. "'Twas even quicker than I thought 'twould be." She winked knowingly. "We'll have to keep a close eye on the nodes, or we'll overshoot Cathbad's time."

He nodded acknowledgment and followed her into the time shaft. He'd have to let go of his anger at Arawn to see his next steps clearly. Knowledge would give him choices, but he had no idea what he'd do with his freedom.

"Doona worry overmuch," she murmured, and he understood she'd been in his head. "When we drop our preconceived notions, the proper course often shows itself."

He held out his arms, and she nestled into them before hunkering next to a wall so she could keep an eye on their location. He remained standing. Good thing because they'd barely gotten going when she barked a word to order the shaft to stop.

"If we were in twelve hundred before, where are we now?" He extended his hands, and she gripped them and flowed to her feet.

"Seven hundred, give or take a few years."

They walked into the dawn of a new day, and he wondered where night had gone. He'd never thought about how the time shaft bent and molded their journey before. He inhaled, filling his lungs with pure, sweet air from an era before men had a chance to pollute it with their ambitious plans for an easier future.

"Aye." A rueful smile made the skin crinkle around her eyes. "I've always loved it in these earlier times, but the Celtic Council picks its location, and the others prefer the comforts of modern life."

"Why not the future? I've gone there a time or two, mostly at Gwydion's behest."

"Och, ye doona wish to know. Some of us check from time to time, but each journey reveals something worse."

"I didn't find it much different from the time I lived in."

"Because ye dinna go far enough forward."

"True. Not more than twenty years or so, though I did catch the front edges of what looked like a major war." Angus wanted to know more, but it's not why they'd come here. "Where's Cathbad?"

"Near the high court of Ulster, I presume." She settled on a large flat rock, and the rising sun glinted off her hair creating a halo effect. Arianrhod patted the granite next to her and began unbraiding her hair, running her fingers through it to smooth it out. "Have a seat."

"Don't we need to be on our way to find Ulster's castle?"

"I have a feeling Cathbad will find us."

Heat rose to his face, and Angus felt foolish. If Cathbad was as powerful as legends portrayed him, he would've dreamed their arrival. He settled next to Arianrhod and took her hand between one of his. "How long do we wait before—"

"Hush." She squeezed his hand before returning to her hair. "Ye canna plan everything. Some things require faith."

The sun was well on its way to the midpoint in the sky, and Angus had shucked his heavy coat, before the sound of horse hooves brought him to his feet. A man rode into sight astride a huge, black destrier. He reined the animal to a halt, and it blew and stamped. Maybe it wanted to run some more.

The man jumped from the horse in an easy movement. Long dark hair framed his sharp-boned face. It hung loose in front, but the back portion was braided close against his skull. Dozens of braids trailed down his back. He was taller than Angus and broad shouldered. Leather garments embellished with red and blue dye clung to his frame like a second skin, and boots laced to just below his knees. A war axe hung from a sheath by his side, and a broadsword was attached to his back by a scabbard with thongs that wrapped around his body. Still more weapons draped from artfully crafted bits of rawhide. He could've been anywhere from thirty to sixty—or much older than that. His face held the same ageless quality that marked the Celtic gods.

He half-bowed toward Arianrhod. "Ye'll excuse us, my lady."

She inclined her head in return and replied, "Of course," before turning away to provide the illusion of privacy.

Angus drew himself tall. It felt important the stranger not find him wanting—in any way. The man approached, staring hard out of eyes the exact shade as Angus's own. Angus felt the man take his measure. He wanted to ask a thousand questions, but remained silent, letting Cathbad set the dynamics for their meeting.

The man raised a hand and placed it on Angus's shoulder. A jolt of something hot and jagged shot through him, and the air took on the tangy scent of the Irish Sea that had to be close.

"I willna apologize for the discomfort." The man tossed his head back and continued to skewer Angus with his hawk-like gaze. "I had to be certain 'twas you returned after all this time."

Angus opened his mouth, but the man shook his head.

"Now isna the time for ye to talk. 'Tis the time for ye to listen."

Angus nodded. The heat running through him from the man's touch intensified, and words rang inside his head.

"As ye surmised, I am Cathbad. Ye are one of my grandsons. Once there was a place for you in Ulster, but ye've been gone a long time."

Angus started to protest that only twenty-five years had passed.

"Twenty-five years for you, but 'tisn't the span of time that's important," Cathbad went on smoothly, obviously tuned into Angus's thoughts. *"Ye have tasks ye must take on in the time where the gods delivered you. 'Tis why ye're there."* He paused and narrowed his eyes, as if considering his next words. *"Ye will return to me, but not for many years."*

Angus couldn't help himself. "Did you know Arawn would hold me in the future?"

Cathbad smiled. *"Aye, laddie. There's little I doona know. Now if ye're asking if he had my blessing to make off with you permanently, the answer is more complicated. In my visions, ye were free to travel betwixt this time and the one where ye find yourself."* A wry chuckle. *"Apparently the Celts werena convinced ye'd welcome their hospitality, so they took a different tack. One which kept you far from me. Ye've been in my vision states, yet I couldna communicate with you that way."*

"Will we be able to meet in the dream world now?"

"Aye. Ye seeking me out dismantled part of the Celts' meddling. She"—he glanced at Arianrhod—*"accomplished the rest of it."*

The conversation held a disjointed feel, so Angus asked questions as they popped into his head. "You haven't exactly said how long it's been since I left here, only that I'll return at some point. How long will you live? For that fact, how long will I?"

"A verra long time."

Angus squared his shoulders. Talking with Cathbad felt very much like consulting an oracle since his answers were far from clear. "What tasks await me?"

"One has already been accomplished, but 'tisn't my place to tell you. Ye must figure it out—and forge a path forward—on your own."

"Surely there's more you can reveal."

Amber eyes bored into him, and Cathbad tightened his grip on Angus's shoulder. *"Much like you, I dream many possibilities. Some come to pass. Others doona. The Celts had one use for you, but mine was far more important. One might say we traded. They used your skills, and I bided my time while ye grew into the role I dreamed for you."*

Angus waited, but Cathbad didn't offer anything further. After a time, he dropped his hand to clasp Angus's. He used a Viking-style grip where his fingers clutched Angus's forearm. Angus copied him. Touching Cathbad healed broken places within him, places where'd he'd felt incomplete, empty.

When Cathbad spoke next, he switched to normal speech. "'Tis essential for a man to know from whence he sprang. 'Tis also important, though not essential, for him to accept the will of the gods. Ye've been angry with the Celts, yet they honed skills ye'd not have gathered had ye remained here."

"That may be, but I don't think I'll ever move past my ill will toward them, no matter what you think they've done for me. Can I ever return here to stay?"

"I already told you that ye'd return, but likely not to remain." He paused. "'Twas wrong for Arawn to hide your origins from you. 'Twasn't part of the bargain I struck, and 'tis why ye feel taken advantage of."

"Thank you. I appreciate you being honest with me."

Cathbad narrowed his eyes. "Is there aught else afore ye find your way back?"

The horse, who'd quieted, returned to blowing and stamping, clearly sensing they'd be leaving soon.

Is there?

"Why was I the one who ended up in the future?"

Cathbad's mouth twitched into half a smile. "Do ye need to ask that? Why do any of us find ourselves where we do?"

Angus felt a sense of peace envelop him. It didn't excuse him from what came next, but it released a part of his power he'd always held in abeyance. The part he'd rode herd on and buried, frightened of its origins. No matter if he didn't remain here. He'd needed to come, to find a link to those who walked before him, to his blood.

Angus smiled, grateful to Cathbad for being plainspoken. "It's enough to know you exist and that I'm of your line."

"Ye've grown wise in the years since ye left." Cathbad's smile broadened, and it transformed the austere planes of his face into something openhearted, rather than harsh. "Ye know where to find me now, lad. The Seer gift runs strong in you. We'll dream one another, now the barriers are down and ye've been here."

The possibility warmed him, connected him to something he'd been missing. "I'd like that."

"Aye then, we'll make certain it happens."

Cathbad released Angus's arm. He walked to his horse and vaulted to its back. Raising a hand in farewell, he cantered off the way he'd come, his back ramrod straight as he sat the horse with an easy grace.

Angus watched until he was out of sight.

Arianrhod turned to face him and settled her multi-hued gaze on his face. He felt her magic probe his mind, but gently, respectfully. "Ye're thinking 'twas worth the detour."

"Aye. Thank you for insisting." He paused, gathering his thoughts as he soaked in the feel of Ulster, the Northern Ireland he'd left behind. "I'm remembering now that I'm here. Many things."

"Good. Those memories are long overdue." She pursed her lips into a disapproving line. "I gathered from listening in on Cathbad's words that Arawn dinna exactly keep his part of the bargain. He must've needed you enough to shroud your mind so ye'd not be able to find your way back."

For the first time, Angus saw things from Arawn's perspective. "Not that it excuses him, but he was afraid I'd bolt at the first opportunity."

"Would ye have?" Arianrhod raised a silver brow.

Angus dug deep and found truth. "Aye, I'd have left if I could. Those first years were hard. Everything was strange, and when I sought my center—to calm myself—all I found was an obstruction. Over the years I got used to the blank spots, so they didn't bother me as much."

"They're gone now." She spoke the words as fact.

He nodded. "I feel whole for the first time since Arawn joined me in the time shaft and used compulsion to expel me through a portal." At the outrage flaring from her eyes, he hurried on. "It's not that he wasn't kind enough. He and Gwydion had a home prepared for me where I was fed and cared for. They came and went, but their tasks for me began immediately. First just dreaming things, but once they were convinced I saw true at least most of the time, they began sending me to fix problems."

She moved in front of him and wrapped her arms around him, tilting her upper body so she still gazed into his face. "Ye have healing energy. 'Tis why they found you so useful. Cathbad radiates the same soothing charm."

Angus snorted. "It didn't feel all that soothing when he was turning my insides to broken glass. Whatever he did made me whole, though, so I'm not complaining." He took a measured breath. "Back to your kin. They wanted me because I could slip into situations, alter them by manipulating earth magic, and leave without much of a trace. So they sent me to do their dirty work. Things they didn't want their name stamped all over."

"Aye, I knew that, but never paid verra much attention." She brushed her thumb over his lower lip, and he kissed her lightly. "I'm sorry. I dinna have the whole story."

He stroked her hair, loving how the silk of it flowed through his fingers. Angus wanted to stay in the bright sunlit glade and make love with her, but they had to warn Eletea before Cavet damaged her beyond redemption. He recalled how distraught she'd been when they first met on the beach near Inishowen. How she'd said she may as well throw herself into one of the craters on Fire Mountain. Not that fire would kill her, but she deserved to find happiness in her beloved Highlands, not the crap Cavet had planned.

Angus laid his cheek alongside Arianrhod's. "We should go."

"Aye, I was just thinking the same thing. Next stop, Rhukon's." She slipped from his arms and chanted to summon a time shaft.

Angus realized with a shock he was looking forward to a confrontation with the dragon shifter. Cathbad's touch had altered something elemental within him, linked him to raw, primal energy that raced through his blood.

She tapped his arm. "Come on. Ye're daydreaming."

"Nay, I'm finally figuring out who I am."

CHAPTER 12

*A*rianrhod brought them out close to the same time they'd left Rhukon's manor house. She aimed for a bit earlier, so perhaps they could confront just him, without Connor or Danne to contend with. Rhukon could always shift to his dragon form, but one dragon was much easier to corral than three.

She watched Angus sidelong. Cathbad had wakened something in him, and she wondered where it would lead. He wasn't the same man who'd fought by her side beneath Rhukon's manor house. Harder. Determined. More sure of himself. And even more appealing to her—if that were possible. What had taken root within him would make it that much more difficult for her to do what she'd eventually have to: return to her life—and position—in the Celtic Pantheon.

She thought about the child. Had Cathbad known about it? She was fairly certain Angus didn't. Not yet anyway. What would he say if he knew?

Angus gripped her elbow. "Now who's daydreaming?"

She turned to face him. Because she was weak where he was concerned, she wrapped her arms around him and let her body melt into his. He cradled her head in his hands and tilted her face back so he could look at her.

"How do you plan to approach Rhukon? Do you have any idea what he and Connor are up to?"

"Aye, and 'tis a good question. Actually two of them."

Ceridwen's words came back to her. *Lachlan and his dragon havena been seen for hundreds of years. They vanished without a trace. Britta and her dragon retreated to an earlier time. We must know if foul energy has infiltrated the dragon shifter bond. If incentives to tempt even the staunchest mage to dark power exist, I would know of them.*

She opened her mouth, but Angus shook his head. "I read your thoughts easily enough. It appears your instructions were far more inclusive than mine. Where I was to determine Eletea's complicity, you were tasked with determining if the evil that's permeated the dragon shifter bond has spread."

"Close enough." She grinned ruefully. "Ceridwen is right about Lachlan and Kheladin, his dragon. No one's seen them since the tail end of the sixteen hundreds. Mayhap they'd be a good starting point."

"You're planning to knock on the front door, waltz in, and have a polite conversation? Ask if he's seen Lachlan lately?" Angus bristled. "After what he did to you?"

"Aye, were ye planning to use magic to knock that same door down?" She furled her brows, but kept talking without waiting for a reply. "Ye wouldna prevail. Rhukon is strong because of his link with Malik. While we're there, I'd like to examine his relationship to Mitha as well. I've thought about who she might be, and there was a minor noblewoman of the same name who shared Rhukon's bed for a time. If we can identify her, betimes we can figure out who her friend is."

"He won't answer any of your questions." Angus's gaze held a hard, flat look.

"Not directly, but mayhap ye can either dig into his mind while I keep him busy with polite conversation, or ye can at least gather enough to dream the truth once we leave."

Angus's eyes widened as the possibilities registered. Clearly, he hadn't considered that alternative. He pressed his lips together. "That would be a new avenue for my power. I haven't used it in quite that way before."

"Consider this good practice."

He shook his head. "I'd rather have practiced before I needed it. This is too important to fuck it up."

She thought about the Morrigan. Shielding her kin ran deep, no matter how annoying they were, but Angus deserved the truth. Straightening, she moved out of his embrace. "I'm not certain, but 'tis possible the Battle Crow has her talons mixed into this mess as well. She always was a pot-stirrer, and she adores conflict. Thrives on it. One of the reasons I'm here is because Mitha was a distant relation of hers, and she pitched a fit about her death at the Celtic Council."

Angus spread his mouth into a cynical smile. "I've avoided the Morrigan up until now. Both Gwydion and Arawn suggested steering clear of that one."

"Wise. She has a long memory and holds grudges. Once when she—"

The blare of dragon hunting cries drowned out her words. Arianrhod craned her neck to look skyward and set her jaw in a resolute line. So much for plans. Two dragons were headed their way. She recognized the black as Malik, but the one with him was a pale ivory shade, something she'd never seen before.

Angus shaded his eyes with a hand and muttered, "What the hell? I had no idea there were white dragons." He raised his dark brows into question marks.

"Neither did I." She sent power scattering skyward, trying to sense if the other dragon was shrouded with some arcane magic she wasn't familiar with.

Not a dragon.

Illusion.

Even though it felt like plunging an appendage into liquid heat that burned worse than a hundred fires, she pressed through the shielding around the white dragon. And wished she'd left well enough alone.

Angus funneled power after hers. A muffled grunt told her the barrier burned him as well. He barked a word that cut the flow of both their magics. Anger flickered in the depths of his eyes. "Funny. We were just talking about her. Why wouldn't she take her own form?"

"Because she likes to play tricks." Arianrhod curled her hands into fists. What in the nine hells was the Morrigan doing masquerading as a dragon?

"I imagine we're about to find out." Angus answered her unspoken question. He stood straighter, hands at his sides, and menace flowed from him.

Arianrhod wound an obfuscation around herself. No matter what else happened today, she didn't want the Morrigan to discover she carried a child conceived by normal means. The Battle Crow would fall on that prime piece of gossip like a starving lion devouring a corpse, and Arianrhod would be forced from the Pantheon into exile. The idea of living out the rest of eternity in Caer Sidi wasn't even marginally appealing, nor would it be an acceptable place for her unborn son. Children needed to be socialized. Living alone with the tides and moon would stunt his potential.

She also didn't want Angus to stumble onto their child by accident. No. That needed to be a private discussion. She'd thought of at least one possibility that included keeping the babe, but hadn't quite worked out all the details, and she needed to before they talked.

First things first. I have to get past the Morrigan afore I can do aught else.

The sound of wingbeats grew louder. As she watched, the white dragon's outline turned indistinct. When the shaded places around it cleared, the Morrigan cawed triumphantly just before she floated to a stop a few feet from Arianrhod and Angus. Another shimmer, and she took on one of her common guises: a crone with tangled black hair, rheumy black eyes, and a long black robe, leaning on an intricately carved staff.

"Isn't this tender," she smirked just before Malik landed heavily and lumbered toward them as he shifted into Rhukon. A buck naked Rhukon, who swaggered to the Morrigan's side.

"Told you we'd see them sooner or later," he said to the Morrigan.

"Nay, 'twas I who told you that." Annoyance roughened the Morrigan's words. She sent a shrewd gaze Arianrhod's way. "What are ye doing here, sister?"

"I could ask you the same thing…sister." The word stuck in Arianrhod's craw, but she used it anyway.

The Morrigan threaded an arm around Rhukon's waist. "Visiting an old friend." Her dark eyes narrowed, and Arianrhod was grateful she'd had the foresight to erect a magical shield. "Unlike some of us, I'm not hampered by virginity."

Arianrhod wanted to snarl that she wasn't *hampered* by being a crow. Angus saved her the trouble. He inclined his head. "Nice to finally meet you. I've heard so much about you from the others."

"Really?" The Morrigan preened beneath his praise, clearly not detecting its mocking nuance.

Rather than answering, Angus strode forward and held out a hand. The Morrigan clasped it, and Rhukon growled his displeasure.

The Morrigan snorted. She winked at Arianrhod, without letting go of Angus's hand. "Men! Aye, and aren't all beasts the same? 'Tis a comely one ye are," she purred meeting Angus's direct gaze. "I can be comely too."

The air around her glistened wetly. When it cleared, she'd reverted to her medieval noblewoman guise. Long dark hair was coaxed into intricate braids, and she regarded Angus out of long-lashed dark eyes. After wetting her full lips with a pink tongue, she bent slightly so her breasts partially spilled from her tightly cut maroon gown.

"He gets to see you this way, and all I get is another dragon?" Rhukon drew his dark brows together until he looked like an angry thundercloud.

"Best watch it," Arianrhod cut in. "Malik will punish you for statements like that."

Smoke rolled from Rhukon's throat. Arianrhod ducked out of the way.

Angus tugged his hand out of the Morrigan's grip. "Do you have an infinite number of forms you can adopt?"

Her dark eyes glittered. "Aye. I can be whatever ye want. Do ye have a preference? Blondes perhaps? Redheads?"

Arianrhod addressed her next words to Rhukon, who was still hissing smoke. "'Tis been many a long year since I've laid eyes on Lachlan. He used to be an associate of yours. Do ye have any idea what's become of him—or his dragon?"

An odd look flitted across Rhukon's shoddily handsome face before he smoothed it away. At least Malik backed off because the smoke stopped. "Why would ye ask me?" Rhukon's tone was carefully neutral.

"I've been asking everyone I come across," Arianrhod countered. "Ceridwen is worried about them."

"Pfft." Rhukon waved a dismissive hand. "Why would she care?"

"She's mother goddess of the world," Arianrhod replied. "She cares about everything."

The Morrigan hadn't taken her gaze from Angus. To annoy her, Arianrhod stepped between them. "Been back to Inverlochy Castle since ye came crying about your distant kinswoman's death...sister?"

"Nay. And ye?"

Arianrhod swallowed back a bitter taste. This was just the sort of sparring the Morrigan loved. Likely she'd visited Rhukon to hatch up more of whatever fueled the poison spreading through the dragon shifters' ranks.

How to either find out more—or get rid of her?

The strategy was so obvious, Arianrhod almost laughed. Instead, she sidled to Angus and murmured. "The Morrigan seems quite taken with you. How about if ye wander off with her? Get to know one another better."

"What a wonderful idea," the Morrigan purred. She closed on Angus, practically pushing Arianrhod to her knees in her hurry, and wrapped a hand around his arm. "Ye heard the lady. Shall we take a stroll?"

Indignation flashed from Angus's eyes, followed by quick understanding as he hooded them to mask his reaction. "Stellar idea," he said and took off at a brisk enough pace, the Morrigan had to trot to keep up.

"Looks like it's just you and me," Arianrhod said brightly to Rhukon. She swept her gaze over him and found a once leanly muscled frame, tending to fat in places. "Ye might want to cut down on those desserts."

He faced her squarely and crossed his arms over his chest. "The Morrigan may be stupid enough to fall for your ploy, but I'm not. Ye can cut the small talk—and the barbed comments. What do ye want?"

She drew herself up to her full height, which rivaled his, and narrowed her eyes. "I want to know what's in it for you."

"What's in what for me? The Morrigan holds power." He licked his full lips in an unmistakable gesture. "And she isna bad in bed."

Arianrhod shook her head. "I could've gone the next century without hearing that. Nay, ye traded something to someone to infuse your dragon shifter bond with dark magic. The thing I canna figure out is why."

"Ye doona know any such thing. So long as we're trading generalities, though, why ask such an obvious question? I thought ye were smarter than that. Dark magic offers so many more possibilities. If I were so inclined, which I'm not."

"Like what?" she pressed.

"Why should I tell you aught else?" he replied sullenly.

She snared him with power and forced his gaze to meet hers. "Because I can offer absolution." It was a huge lie, but he didn't need to know that. About all she could offer was time without end moldering away in the *Dreaming*.

He skinned his lips back, baring his teeth in a snarl. "Why would I want or need *absolution?*" His dark eyes blazed with barely-leashed fury.

"Ye havena faced Ceridwen's wrath. She might just upend you into that cauldron of hers." Arianrhod kept the heat up to chivvy him into making a mistake. Rhukon was egotistical enough, he might let something slip if he got mad.

"Not verra bloody likely."

"Ye dinna answer me about Lachlan." Arianrhod focused compulsion in a stream that broke over Rhukon's head.

He must've felt it because he blinked furiously and glared at her. His snarl widened. Magic bubbled around him as he instigated the shift back to Malik's form. "Ye'll never find him or that young buck dragon of his, either," Malik shouted in a shower of flames that sent cinders to burn holes in her battle leathers.

She tried to rescind the transition and force Rhukon back to his body, but the dragon magic was too strong. She was still trying when the black dragon spread his wings and took to the skies, braying laughter.

"Stupid Celt," was his parting shot.

"Fuck!" She stamped her foot, but it wasn't enough to dissipate her anger, so she picked up a good-sized rock and chucked it as far as she could. She thought about following Rhukon back to his manor house, but recognized the futility in that approach. He knew where Lachlan was, though. He'd looked guilty as sin, even though he hadn't actually admitted anything.

Likely that's not good for Lachlan.

She glanced around for Angus and the Morrigan, but empty countryside—wet, verdant, and uninhabited—stretched as far as she could see. Jealousy sent a lance into her heart. Sure, the Morrigan looked like a slutty tavern wench, but Angus would be able to see through that, wouldn't he?

What if she ensorcels him?

She could. Her magic is far stronger and more ancient than his.

Arianrhod wrapped her arms around herself, suddenly chilled to her bones. She didn't think he'd do anything stupid, but he was a man, and men thought with their cocks. It was a very old story.

Standing still didn't dispel the nervous energy thrumming through her, so she took off at a long-legged pace without any destination in mind. She needed an opportunity by herself to think about the life that grew within her, and this would be as good as any other.

What the hell was she going to do?

The easiest course of action would be to deny the child a chance at life. After getting saddled with Dylan and Lleu—even though there was no way she could've avoided the magic behind their making—she should've taken precautions. She'd never bothered with her dragon lover because their disparate DNA couldn't have produced viable offspring.

What was the problem this time?

The question was rhetorical. She knew exactly what the problem had been. She'd been so swept up in the heat that ignited between them, so drawn in by wanting Angus, the last thing on her mind was babies.

She splayed a hand across her abdomen, feeling protective toward the threads of life taking root inside her. She sifted her hands through her hair. This wasn't a time to get maudlin. Even if she could get away with slipping out of sight long enough to carry the child and wean it, no way could she devote years to raising it.

Would Angus want to?

She had no idea. He'd likely be disappointed or angry or passive aggressive as hell when she told him she couldn't share anything that looked like a normal life with him. Not that she didn't want to, but it wasn't her destiny. At least not right now. She saw that clearly standing in the middle of eighteenth century moorland. Why hadn't it been this obvious before?

She glanced around again, still not finding a trace of Angus or the Morrigan. Where the hell had they gotten off to? Try as she might, she couldn't envision Angus falling for the Battle Crow's cheap wiles, but he was a man after all.

If he got sidetracked this easily by the Morrigan, he won't want the child, either.

Nay, one doesna follow from the other. I'm just jealous because he went off with her—never mind 'twas my suggestion.

I doona have any idea what he wants or doesna want. I doona know him well enough.

A flat rock in the sun beckoned. She sat heavily on it and supported her head in one hand. Part of her thought she should return to Inverlochy Castle, report in, and be done with things. Before she could act on it, the sun warmed her chilled places, and her eyes fluttered shut.

She felt the beginnings of a vision in a particular lightness in her midsection. Expecting a message from Ceridwen or another of the Celts, she opened herself. Shock roiled through her when Cathbad stood framed in her third eye.

"Goddess." He inclined his head.

"Seer." She gazed into eyes identical to Angus's.

"Ye must keep the child," he said without preamble. "He has a crucial role to play in what's to come."

She didn't waste words asking how he knew. "I've been trying to see my way clear to do that. It willna be easy."

"Ye have the answers ye need. Angus will raise his son."

"How can ye be so certain he'll agree?"

"How can ye be certain he willna?" With a broad wink, Cathbad's figure fragmented into a million motes of light, and her mind was her own again.

Arianrhod glanced at the sun tracking its way to the western horizon. Though it didn't seem possible, she'd lost at least an hour. Maybe more. Footsteps pounding toward her brought her to her feet.

"There you are," Angus cried and ran hard right for her. "You didn't stay where I left you." Mild accusation ran beneath his words.

She looked behind him. "Where's the Morrigan?"

He rolled his eyes and laughed. "I kept up a pretense long enough to glean what I could. Once I knew I couldn't get any more, I became distant enough she got angry and left."

"Do ye think she went back to Rhukon's?"

"Aye, that's exactly what I think, but I don't want to talk about her." He held out his arms, and she walked into them and wrapped hers around him. "Miss me?" He kissed the top of her head.

"I shouldna admit it, but aye."

He tightened his arms around her. "You were right about the Morrigan being up to her wings in the dragon shifter mess." He paused a beat. "She's rather like a combination of cheerleader and advice maven, suggesting they try things to sink themselves in even deeper. She alluded to others she was working with too, powerful beings she wouldn't name."

"'Twould be verra like something she'd do. I got Rhukon—well actually Malik—to admit he knows about Lachlan's disappearance."

"Who was Lachlan exactly?"

"One of the good dragon shifters. He and his dragon, Kheladin, havena been seen since the late sixteen hundreds. I dinna get a chance to ask after Britta and Tarika, two others who've been scarce, though I suspect they're deep in Fire Mountain, or else hiding out somewhere in a time period where they doona expect to be disturbed. Tarika is one of the First Borns, and she wouldna allow herself—or her dragon shifter mage—to become trapped by another's magic."

Angus stroked firm hands down her back. "Do you want to confront Rhukon further?"

Arianrhod thought about it and shook her head. She played with the spill of hair down his shoulders, enjoying the texture between her fingers. "Nay. Nothing to be gained, unless we held him down and tortured him. And I doubt we could do so. The dragon would gain ascendency and fry us with fire."

The hands on her back moved to her hair, and he laced his fingers into its weave. "We still need to warn Eletea. Do you suppose they'll allow us into Fire Mountain, given how they kicked us out last time?"

"We must try. I believe they'll be verra interested in any information at all about Lachlan. His dragon Kheladin was young, but quite a favorite among the First Borns."

He brushed his lips over hers and moved to her side, where he draped an arm around her shoulders. They walked toward where the time shaft had spit them out. It was a wise move, since she felt drained.

"Once we're done with Fire Mountain,"—he snugged his grip on her waist, drawing her closer—"I'm looking forward to an uninterrupted stretch of time alone with you."

She nodded, not trusting herself to speak. She wanted the same, more than anything, and it scared her to death. She couldn't become dependent on the man by her side. Missing him would make the next stretch of years even more unbearable than the last few thousand had been.

"What?" he asked softly.

"Nothing. I'm just tired."

CHAPTER 13

*A*ngus settled into a crouch in the time shaft and cradled Arianrhod in his arms, so she could lean against his spread knees. He'd listened to her account of her time with Rhukon, and now it was his turn to talk about the Morrigan. He blew out a breath.

The Battle Crow made him feel dirty. All she'd wanted to do was fuck him, but once she got him inside her body, he suspected she'd weave some arcane magic to enslave him. He thought he'd be strong enough to resist, yet he hadn't been totally certain. Besides, the thought of having sex with her made him vaguely ill, and he hated the idea of another woman anywhere near him after the wonder of Arianrhod. With all the Morrigan's shapeshifting, for all he knew, she wasn't anything beyond a shapeless blob of protoplasm.

"Take your time," Arianrhod murmured. "She'd rattle the best of us."

He laughed uncomfortably. "Aye, I figured I was one lucky son of a bitch to get out of there with both balls." He hesitated, then opted for honesty. "At first, she was so closed to me, I wondered what I'd have to do to get into her mind, but it turned out touching her hand and arm gave me plenty." A disgusted tremor tracked down his body. "I don't think I could've stood to get much closer than that. She had this smell, like something ill, but not quite dead."

"I know that smell. I always figured it came from the carrion she eats in her raven form. That one's always made my skin crawl, but I've hidden my reaction from her. She's such a bully, if she knew about my antipathy, she'd taunt me with it." Arianrhod shivered in his arms, and he sent soothing energy into her.

"I've upset you. Would you rather I craft a facile story?" he asked.

She shook her head. "Nay. I always prefer truth. The only reason she wants you is because she's obsessed with controlling everyone and everything she comes across, but 'tisn't of any import. What did ye find out?"

"The dragon shifter mages embraced dark magic, so they could drain power from their dragons and make themselves not only immortal, but invincible."

Arianrhod shifted in his arms until she faced him, and both of them settled gingerly on what passed for a floor in the time shaft. It was soft and spongy, and Angus took care not to disturb what was likely living flesh any more than he had to.

A vertical crease formed between Arianrhod's brows as she frowned. "Did ye determine just how the Morrigan is wrapped up in this?"

"Did I ever. It was her plan in the first place, but since her power is limitless—and she knew Ceridwen would never stand by while she alienated the dragons—she needed others to experiment with. They weren't easy to find. Most of the dragon shifters adore their dragons."

"Did ye discover if there are others beyond Rhukon and Connor?"

"Nay. I was fortunate to see what I did. She underestimated the extent of my magic because she was so busy trying to seduce me."

"Och, what a meddling bitch she is." Arianrhod clamped her teeth over her lower lip. "I doona suppose this is a topic we could bring afore the Council. She'd deny it—and then she'd target you for destruction, and not in an easy way, either."

"Death by fucking." He rolled his eyes and laughed.

"'Tisn't funny."

"Probably not." He thought about it and added, "This is one instance where we can accomplish more from behind the scenes than marching through the front door."

She moved one hand in a circular motion. "Say more."

"We start with Eletea—assuming we can find her—and address this one dragon at a time. Even if the Celts might be swayed by the Morrigan, the dragons will be very interested to hear from the two of us."

Her frown deepened. "We'll have to pick carefully. Otherwise, word will filter back to Ceridwen and she'll be furious we dinna go through her first."

"You may report to her, but I report to Arawn. I suspect he'd feel the same way. Unfortunately, he wouldn't be angry enough to banish me. I'm too useful."

Arianrhod bristled. "I doona work for Ceridwen. I merely give her information as a courtesy."

Amusement danced beneath the surface as he replied, "I'll keep it in mind."

She took his hand. "Ye'd be wise to do that. We havena talked of your relationship with the Celts. Now that ye know about Cathbad, what will ye do?"

He pushed anger at how the Celts had used him aside. She'd asked an important question, and he didn't have a fully formed answer. Not yet, anyway. He glanced at a passing node to see how much more time they had.

None.

He got to his feet and pulled her upright along with him. "I'm not sidestepping your question, but it's time to go." He chanted and the pulsing gray-pink walls shuddered to a halt. The opening he expected was slow to form, and Arianrhod pushed magic after his to force things along.

Finally, a wall split, allowing them to exit. "'Twould appear we've either worn out our welcome in the shaft, or the dragons instructed it not to allow us entry," Arianrhod observed dryly and made her way through the portal. He followed her out into an inky moonless night with thick clouds riding overhead. The ever-present heat of Fire Mountain closed around him.

"We need to finish talking," he said, but it'll have to wait until we're done here."

Arianrhod leaned close, but used shielded mind speech anyway. *"Do ye wish to speak with a select dragon or two about the dark mages co-opting dragon magic?"*

He thought about it. *"Let's see if they stonewall us finding Eletea, and then we can decide."*

He took stock of where they were. For once, not too far from the mound that housed the dragons' council chambers. He reached for her hand, but she shook her head, and he felt her wrap magic around herself. Before he could wonder why, he caught sight of a green dragon winging its way toward them. Probably the same one who'd dismissed them from this world. Angus straightened his spine and clasped his hands behind his back, waiting.

The dragon touched down lightly and focused her whirling gaze on Angus and Arianrhod. "What are you doing back here?" The words were harsh, clipped. She didn't bother masking her annoyance.

"We must speak with Eletea," Arianrhod said, standing tall as she faced off against the dragon. "She's in danger."

"We can take care of our own." The dragon bristled.

"I never said ye couldna." Arianrhod's voice was soft, laced with compulsion. "Would ye rather I told you, and then ye could take it from there?"

Wingbeats drew Angus's gaze skyward. Another dragon, this one copper, flew toward them. Was it Eletea? He sent power spiraling outward to detect who was heading for them and smiled. In the brief time he'd spent with the young, earnest dragon, he'd come to care about her.

"Hold." He addressed Arianrhod. "You can tell her yourself."

She glanced up, right along with the green dragon, who clanked her jaws together in what sounded like exasperation.

"I'm glad ye dinna imprison her." Arianrhod threw down the gauntlet by saying what Angus was thinking.

"We don't *imprison* our own unless there's need," the green gritted out.

Eletea landed heavily a few feet away and trudged toward them kicking fist-sized stones out of her way with her large back feet. She looked sad, resigned, and years older than when Angus first met her.

"Good to see you." He strode toward her wanting to hug her, but dragons didn't lend themselves to hugging. "How are your wings mending?"

She held up a foreleg when he was two feet away, clearly meaning for him to stop. "It's kind of you to ask. They're fine now. We have healers among us, and they helped repair the mutilation."

He wanted to ask about the damage to her spirit, but since the message he'd come to deliver about Cavet would make things worse, he settled for, "I'm glad."

"Thank you for rescuing me. I didn't get a chance to tell you before." She shifted her gaze to Arianrhod and bowed her head. "You too, goddess."

"We do not bow to the Celts," the green hissed.

Eletea drew herself to her full height, which was a foot shorter than the green dragon. "I can take things from here, Dorae. You needn't trouble yourself."

The green dragon puffed steam and smoke before spreading her wings and taking to the skies. Angus gazed after it. "How'd you get her to leave without pitching a fuss?" he asked Eletea.

"One dragon can't refuse a reasonable request from another," she replied. "I've been cleared in Mitha's death, so Dorae couldn't turn me down." Eletea puffed flames skyward. "Well, she could've, but it would have been terribly rude."

"At least we know her name," Angus said. "She never told us."

"Never mind her." Eletea crossed her forelegs over her copper-scaled chest. "Did you return to Rhukon and Connor? Are they dead?" She leaned forward, her eyes a whirlwind of menace, mingled with fury.

"Aye, we returned, yet they are verra much alive, I fear," Arianrhod replied.

"I didn't realize the dragons had exonerated you about Mitha, so when I couldn't get the truth of things from Rhukon and Connor, I dreamed it," Angus broke in. He hunted for a softer spin to describe his vision, but gave up. "You won't like what I have to say."

"How much worse could it be than Rhukon and Connor wanting me dead?" she countered. "Or Danne's betrayal? You're fortunate you caught me here. I'll be returning to Cavet and the Highlands at first light. He's anxious for me to come home."

"About that—" Angus began, faltered, and cleared his throat.

"What?" Eletea marched closer and bent her head until she was nose to nose with him. "Say what you will, Seer."

"You can certainly return to the Highlands, but I'd forget about Cavet."

Eletea blanketed him with steam. "I'll do no such thing. I know the others think he's a ladies' dragon, but he's never given me cause not to trust him."

"You must listen to me," Angus persisted, afraid if he didn't get the words out, Eletea would leave. "Please. My visions are true seeing. Cavet and Danne plotted together. Danne told him Mitha had a friend who wished to form a shifter bond with him. Both dragons assumed the dark magic would empower them, but what they didn't realize is it opens a conduit for the mage to drain their magic."

A high, shrieking moan rose from Eletea, followed by a blast of fire that singed the small hairs lining Angus's nose. The dragon collapsed into a heap, tears turning to gemstones as they scattered about her.

Arianrhod walked to Angus and reached out with a hand. After a brief hesitation, she laid it on Eletea's scaled hide. "'Tis sorry I am," she crooned. "He doesna deserve you."

The dragon's head snapped up. "If your next words will be about me finding someone else to love, I don't want to hear them." Smoky snot flowed from her nose and she shook it to the ground as she shifted her wounded eyes to Angus. "I want to dismiss what you told me, chalk it up to misinterpretation, yet I heard truth in your words."

Thanks be to the gods.

Angus was grateful beyond reckoning he didn't have to launch a convoluted explanation of how his vision states tapped into reality. Far better for the dragon to accept his words, painful though they had to be. Maybe he wouldn't have to tell her the part about Cavet planning to spread vicious lies about her among her kin.

"What will ye do?" Arianrhod asked the dragon the same question she'd asked him in the time shaft.

"Do you have any idea who the other human mage was?" Eletea asked Angus. When he shook his head, she went on, "Pity. Too bad Danne's dead. He never could keep secrets for long, and I could've trapped him into telling me."

"Why bother?" Arianrhod narrowed her eyes. "Ye might be better served to move on."

"I wish to remain in the Highlands, which means Cavet must leave."

Angus opened his mouth to tell her the Highlands were a big place, but shut it when he realized dragons covered far more real estate than humans. He turned to Arianrhod. "It would be useful to know who the other woman is—"

"Woman!" Eletea screeched. "Another mixed-sex dragon shifter pair! What heresy. We must find out who it is. I'll kill her too."

"I have a feeling I can find out." Angus spoke slowly, thinking of information he'd stolen from the Morrigan.

"How?" Eletea all but pounced on him with both forelegs. "If the dark mages wish to drain dragons of their power, I need to let the Council know. I never cared for Malik or Preki, but the Council must sever their bonding—"

Arianrhod held up a hand. "Stop. Else we'll be at cross purposes. As I see it, we have three problems." She ticked them off on her fingers. "One, Cavet. Two, the unknown woman who wishes to become a dragon shifter. Three, the plot to siphon off dragon magic to strengthen the dark mage dragon shifters."

Eletea straightened from her slump. "I'll take care of that last one. I'll tell the Council and let them test all the dragon shifter pairs."

"While ye're at it," Arianrhod said, "Rhukon knows where Lachlan is, but wouldn't tell me. My guess is Lachlan and his dragon met with foul play."

"They can't be dead," Eletea protested. "They're immortal."

"Aye, but they can be ensorcelled. 'Tisn't so different from death."

Angus felt proud of how Eletea had rallied, despite what must be crushing disappointment and a broken heart. "We'll take care of sorting out who Mitha's friend is."

Eletea's eyes whirled faster. "Maybe I can do that too. I'll return to Cavet, pretend I know nothing, and give him many opportunities to make a mistake." She lowered her voice. "He isn't very smart. I've known that ever since I joined him, but…" Her voice trailed off, and she dropped her gaze, looking embarrassed

"Are there dragons you trust on the Council?" Angus asked.

"Certainly."

"Well then," he continued, "you might tell them about Cavet and set up reinforcements in the Highlands if you plan to spy on him."

"I can do that," Eletea said. "Do you know why the mages want to fill themselves with dragon power?"

Angus shook his head. "It might be as simple as wanting power for its own sake, though. Often that's the case."

"I like the idea of Eletea bringing other dragons with her to the Highlands." Arianrhod spoke up. "If we get verra lucky, they'll dispatch Cavet and the one who wants to bond with him—if we doona locate her first."

"Thank you. I'll do my part to bring Cavet to justice. Those wiser than me will work to weed out whatever is poisoning the dragon shifter bond." Eletea stretched a foreleg toward Angus, and he grasped one of her talons. She did the same with Arianrhod. "I'll be on my way." She swept a wingtip to the side. "You're both welcome in Fire Mountain so long as I live. Let no dragon say otherwise."

Angus tilted his head and watched her disappear from view. "She's got spirit."

"Aye that she does. 'Tis time for us to get going too."

He gathered her into his arms and pressed his lips against her forehead. "Where shall we go?"

She laid her cheek in the hollow between his neck and shoulder and wound her arms around him. "Assuming the time-travel shaft is over its snit, we could either go to my house or yours."

"If you want privacy, we should pick yours. Arawn and Gwydion gifted me my lodgings. Most of the time, they leave me alone, but if they want something, they wander in as if the place were theirs."

"Mmph. Afore we leave here, do ye have any ideas about who Mitha's associate might be?"

"Nay, but I spent enough time with the Morrigan, I can work a dream state to pick through what I might have missed." He paused a beat, not certain of his next words. "Cathbad said we might share dreaming. He's much more powerful than me. Perhaps, if I call on him—"

"—he can come up with more," she finished before he could get the words out and ran her hands down his back. "Brilliant! I love it."

The ground rumbled beneath their feet. "Oh for fuck's sake, stop that." Angus let go of her long enough to shake his fist at the vibrating surface, and it quieted. "Son of a bitch." He tightened his hold on her once more. "Makes a man feel powerful."

"Ye are powerful." She spoke into his ear. "More than ye realize."

He angled his head and gazed into her face until emotion threatened to choke him. Words forced their way past years of self-imposed control. "You feel amazing in my arms, Ari. I'm falling in love with you."

Her body, so pliant and fluid a moment before, stiffened in his arms. A curtain dropped over her eyes extinguishing their warmth, and she shook her head sadly. "Not a sound idea. I'm not a good bet." She let go of him. "Come on, let's get out of here."

CHAPTER 14

She was afraid to say anything else. Afraid if she opened her mouth, she'd tell him she loved him right back. And then where would they be? Locked into something impossible. That's where. She wrapped her arms around herself and settled into the time shaft to wait out the journey. Just their luck this was one of the longer jaunts.

Time slid past, and she began to hope he'd let the subject drop. He faced half away from her, and when she cast sidelong glances his way, his forehead was creased in thought and his eyes were shut.

When he broke the silence, his voice startled her. "What do you mean *not a good bet*? Why not?"

She swallowed around a dry throat, not wanting to have this conversation. "I already told you."

"If it's that damned virgin huntress thing—" he began.

"'Tisn't a thing." Her voice rose, but she couldn't rein it in. "'Tis who I am. I doona ken why ye doona respect me or my standing in the Pantheon."

"Fuck the Celts," he roared and drove a fist into one of the pulsing walls of the shaft.

Reaction was immediate. The shaft ground to a halt, split along one side, and threw both of them out. She landed on her belly and rolled to a sit, cursing. Water from very wet earth soaked into her leathers. The sun was heading for the western horizon, which meant late afternoon. At least it wasn't raining.

Angus groaned from where he lay a few feet away, half on his back, half on one side. After a long moment, he hoisted himself to a crouch. "Don't say a word." He shot a guilty glance her way. "I shouldn't have done that. Do you have any idea where we are?" He sniffed audibly. "Not home. The air's too clean."

She got to her feet, grateful she still had her bow and quiver. "Nay, but I can figure it out easily enough. Give me a moment." By the time she cast a cautious spell to gather data, he was on his feet and making his way to her side.

"Best I can tell"—she smiled grimly—"we're around eighty years shy of our own time, and we're in Northern Ireland."

He set his jaw in a harsh line. "Good thing it's not a few years later. We'd be square in the middle of that unholy mess when the IRA took on the Brits. Again. I'm sorry. That was incredibly stupid. How can I make amends to whatever operates the time-traveling mechanism?"

"I have no idea where to even begin to figure that out."

"We could hunt down the other Celts. Someone would likely know."

"Let's save that for a last resort." She raised her arms above her head to stretch out the sore places from hitting the ground when the shaft ejected her. "The first thing my kin will want to know is how ye came to lose your temper."

He closed on her and gripped her upper arms. "About that, lass—"

"I doona wish to speak of it."

"Oh you don't, do you? Too bad. I do, and we will."

She wrenched out of his grip and drew back a hand to slap him. He caught it in midair. "No man orders me about." She yanked at her hand, but he held firm. "Let go of me." She yanked harder and summoned magic until light danced beneath her skin, spilling from her in an iridescent flood.

"Arianrhod." He spoke her name like a prayer, a benediction. "Please. Talk with me."

She stopped struggling and looked hard at him through the prism of her power. The light in his eyes was wounded, yet hopeful —and determined. Anger bled from her. When he held out his arms, she came into them.

He stroked her hair, and she listened to the steady beat of his heart, feeling as if she were being torn in two. She wanted him, ached for him. He must've sensed her yearning because he angled her head and crushed his mouth over hers. Desperation and heat kindled a sexual bonfire, turning her nerves into a million points of sensation. The light streaming from her intensified.

Angus forced her mouth open and plumbed it with his tongue. She sucked hungrily on him, pretending she held his cock in her mouth. As if it heard her thoughts, his ridged flesh swelled against her belly, and she forced a hand between them to curve around it. Breath caught in her throat, and her heart hammered against her ribs.

They stood twined together, kissing and touching one another as long moments stretched past. He thrust into her hand and she straddled one of his legs, pressing her inflamed center against his thigh. Finally, she wrenched her mouth from his, breathing hard.

"We need—" He glanced around them, probably seeking respite from the waterlogged ground.

"Aye. Look over there." She pointed. "'Tis the best we'll find on short notice." Letting go of him, she made her way to a tumble of sun-warmed stones and funneled magic to warm them still more. "'Tisn't perfect, but 'twill do so long as no one ventures by." She busied her fingers with the fastenings of his breeches and drew his cock out. He made a decidedly male sound when she worked him with her hand and bent to lick drops of semen off him.

He fondled her breasts through her shirt, rolling her nipples between his fingers. Sparks shot straight to her pussy. Already wet, another gush pulsed between her legs, and she hovered on the edge of an orgasm. He moved a hand between her legs, rubbing hard, and brought her over the edge. She cried his name and writhed against his fingers.

Arianrhod let go of him and undid the laces holding her trousers in place. She pushed them down her legs, along with her drenched smallclothes, and bent over the flat rock she'd warmed with magic.

Behind her, Angus gasped, "Gods, but you're lovely," just before he surged inside her. He settled his hands on her waist and drove himself until he was fully encased in her body. She tilted her hips to improve the angle and rocked against him urging him to move, fast and hard, but all he did was twitch his cock inside her, making her nerve endings scream for more.

She tried to move, but he held her fast. When she was within a hairsbreadth of begging, he withdrew very slowly, swirled the head of his cock in a circular motion around her opening, and pressed back inside. Around the third or fourth long, slow stroke, he settled one of his hands between her legs and teased her nub with knowing fingers.

The song he'd sung before rose around her, the notes poignant, evocative, laden with seduction and unslaked lust. She raised her voice to join him and magic shimmered in the air, turning it to molten silver around them.

She melted into another orgasm, followed by one more. He drove into her faster, and the cadence of his breathing quickened, became more ragged as music rose and fell around her. Even though she couldn't see him, she knew his nipples were hard and his balls snugged against his body. He teased and tweaked her clit, stopping and starting, forcing her to ride the edge of another peak. His cock swelled inside her, and he gave up any pretense of control.

Music spiraled everywhere, joining colors in a kaleidoscopic display. The spasms of his release rocked her, and she convulsed around him. Long moments passed before she came back into herself.

After a final, playful twitch, he pulled his still-erect cock from her body and tugged her upright. Angus turned her to face him and kissed her gently before bending to coax her small clothes and trousers back up her legs. She worked on her laces while he jockeyed himself back into his breeches and did them up.

Love streamed from him, picking up the silvery motes that still danced in the air and spinning them in joyful aerial displays. He tipped her chin with one hand so she had to look at him. "How can you walk away from this?"

"I doona know if I can, but I had a thought. Two actually." She sucked in a nervous breath. What she was about to ask held risks. For one, he'd find out about their child, but he'd have to sometime.

"I'm listening." His expression was so solemn, it tugged at her heart.

"The first is easy. If we bide a bit more here, 'tis possible, the time shaft will allow us back inside. We canna be the first who've misbehaved in its folds."

He sent a bawdy wink skittering across the short distance between them. "And how shall we while away the waiting time?"

Arianrhod rolled her eyes. "Men! Not that I wouldn't love to wrap myself in your body and never surface, but if we can find a place to build a fire, mayhap ye can dream if we have a future. While ye're there, ye can hunt for Mitha's accomplice."

"I've never asked the visions for two separate things."

"Does that mean 'tisn't possible?"

He shrugged. "I don't know. If I have to enter a trance twice, it will take longer, but that's not the end of the world. First off," he cast his gaze around them, "we need to find somewhere we can settle for a while."

"I've already looked. Shepherds' huts dot the hills above us. Many are empty now, but I canna tell if their owners' return is imminent."

He held out a hand to her. "Let's find out."

She grasped it and walked beside him up a steep, muddy hillside. Whatever the oracle—or whoever gave him his visions—revealed would determine much. Walking away would've been far safer and more prudent.

Except she couldn't do it.

~

"Over there." Angus pointed at a small stone hut with a sod roof, clearly left over from the sixteen or seventeen hundreds. "Part of the roof's falling in, but the hearth could be intact. At least we can be confident no one will bother us."

"Heather and gorse will give us something to burn—once we dry them out."

"Maybe we'll get lucky and there'll be a sod block or two inside."

She elbowed him. "Are ye always this optimistic?"

His smile vanished, replaced by a webbing of fine lines around his eyes and a thoughtful expression. "I wasn't optimistic at all—until I met you." More words wanted out, but he smothered them. Last time he told her he loved her, she had a meltdown, and she still hadn't exactly told him why.

Maybe if I was one of the gods, I'd understand what her position in the Pantheon means to her.

They reached the hut and he stepped over a high sill into the small, dark space. The piece of animal hide that had once covered the opening had long since moldered to dust. Bats squealed and brushed against him in their hurry to exit. He looked for mice, but didn't find any. The piquant, peppery smell of bat guano tickled his nostrils. The floor was inches deep in the stuff.

"Och, and 'tis a wee bit close in here." Arianrhod moved to his side. She still glowed from their lovemaking, but she summoned her mage light and cast it about the hut. A recessed hole at one end had once been a fire pit. Blackened stones rose above it to the low ceiling.

Angus kicked a path to the pit and brushed a clear place in front of it. Once he had a reasonably clean place to kneel, he craned his neck to look up the flue. Arianrhod's light obligingly floated a few inches up the dark outlet shaft.

"Here." She handed him what had once been the handle to something. Though it was splintered off at one end, it was still a stout length of wood. He jammed it into the opening until debris cascaded into an untidy heap. Dust rose, and he covered his nose and mouth with a bent elbow. When he bent to look next, he saw daylight at the other end.

"All we need now is tinder," he said.

"All this bat shit"—she kicked at it—"should help."

He stared at it. "How?"

"'Tis rich in nitrate. I believe 'twas used in gunpowder at some point."

Angus grinned. "Guess there's something to be said for being old —and having access to your memories."

She laughed, and the sound warmed him. "Never tell a woman she's old." Arianrhod made her way toward the opening.

"I'll try to remember that. Where are you going?"

"We'll still need tinder. 'Twill smell bad enough in here burning bat shit. Best to break it up with wood."

It took them until shadows gathered across the moors to round up what they needed for a fire. Angus kept an anxious eye out for other people, but he hadn't sensed a soul close by since they arrived.

"Best get to it," he said to bolster his confidence. He wanted to know about his future with Arianrhod, but what if the answers weren't what he hoped?

A small jolt told him she'd been inside his head. "Aye," she concurred. "I want answers as well."

He narrowed his eyes. "Surely Bran, god of prophecy, could serve as seer when you have need to scry the future."

"Aye, but he's a terrible gossip. Worse than the Morrigan for spreading juicy bits about." Arianrhod shook her head, and her hair brushed the dirt floor they'd taken time to clear. A mound of bat guano sat near the hearth. "Ye're stalling."

He was. Angus focused a trickle of magic to light the tinder piled in the hearth. It caught, smoking a bit before it developed a life of its own. He shucked his jacket and rolled up his shirtsleeves. Next he tugged his dirk from its waist sheath and drew it down both forearms. Once blood flowed, he held his arms over the blaze, waiting for his essence to blend with the fire.

When it came, the trance hit with such force his head snapped backward, and he nearly lost his balance. The air glistened wetly around him, and he breathed the metallic scent of power deep into his lungs, displacing the rancid stench of burning bat shit.

He readied his questions, waiting.

"Grandson!" Cathbad wavered into view.

"Sire." Angus bowed. "I'd thought of calling for you, but hadn't yet."

"I knew ye'd have need of me. Once I felt your energy, I summoned a trance state. Our time will be short. Ask what ye will."

"Tell me of Arianrhod. Do we have a future together?"

Cathbad narrowed his eyes. "Aye and nay."

Angus waited, wanting to shake truth out of his kinsman, yet understanding strong emotion would unravel the vision. Having made that mistake in the time shaft, he wasn't anxious to repeat it.

"Good ye're not peppering me with questions." Cathbad nodded approvingly. "She carries your child—"

"That's excellent news!" Angus wanted to whoop, turn cartwheels for the joy surging through him, but positive emotions could undo the trance too.

"Ye havena heard the rest. She must hide from her people long enough to carry and wean your son, then she will bring him to you to raise."

Angus sorted through Cathbad's words. "Why can't we live as a couple? Raise him together."

"'Tisn't what I've seen." He hesitated a beat then went on. "The boy is important. He has a critical role to play. Ye must do this. Ye havena a choice."

"Will Arianrhod and I ever get a chance to live together openly? To marry?"

Cathbad hesitated, then said, "Such hasna been given to me to know. Not yet, anyway. Hold hope, though. 'Tis always possible."

A welter of emotions pummeled Angus, but he couldn't let any of them out to play. "I will fulfill my part."

"'Twill mean ye'll continue as ye've been, living with the Celts and working whatever tasks they send your way."

Angus was aware of his blood flowing faster, blending with the flames. "Will I ever see an end to that?"

"Aye. Once the boy is raised, ye'll find the peace ye seek."

"But not with Arianrhod."

Cathbad shook his head and his hair settled around him, glinting with blue-black highlights. "I dinna say that. Truthfully, I doona know. Is there aught else? My time grows short."

Angus sketched out the problem of the unknown dark mage who wished to become a dragon shifter.

"Let the dragons handle their own problems," Cathbad said. "They're good at it, and ye run the risk of them accusing you of meddling unless they've specifically directed you to do something."

Angus nodded. Cathbad's form developed shimmery edges, and Angus said, "Wait."

"Aye, what? I'm nearly at the end of my energy."

"Have my dreams always come from you?"

"Nay. Only today, and only because I joined my energy with yours. Our trances are Danu's gift. Call me into your visions if ye have need."

Cathbad's image flickered and faded along with his words; the trance dissipated along with him.

Angus pitched to his knees and sent power to sever his connection with the fire. Blood dried on his forearms, and he summoned healing energy to mend his cuts. Now that he didn't have to ride herd on his emotions, raw joy shot through him. How wondrous to have a child to raise. It would make whatever the Celts dealt out more palatable and shift an alien land into a home.

Arianrhod knelt behind him and cradled him in her arms.

When he could form words, he twisted to face her. "Why didn't you tell me about our son?"

CHAPTER 15

*T*here were so many things she wanted to ask, her head was bursting with holding them back. She'd wanted to peek into Angus's trance, but worried she'd ruin something if she shoehorned her energy into things.

"Why didn't you tell me about our son?" he repeated, his gaze trained on hers. Golden flecks shimmered around his pupils.

"I wasna certain what I wanted to do." Because she couldn't stand the sudden desolation behind his eyes—a product of her honesty—she hurried on. "Cathbad paid me a visit while ye were with the Morrigan. He told me our child was predestined, important in ways he dinna elucidate. 'Twas then I knew I'd take the hard road, bear our son, and deal with consequences as they arose."

"Did Cathbad also tell you that I'd raise him—alone?"

Arianrhod nodded solemnly. "I owe you an apology for even considering not telling you."

A rough expression, feral and untamed, hardened his features into a mask. "Aye, that you do, but we can't go back."

"Nay, we canna." She forced herself to hold his gaze. He was so forthright, she couldn't meet him with less than he gave. "Let's start with the easy parts. What did ye find out about the dark mage dragon shifters?"

Angus nodded and altered his position, so he could wrap his arms around her. He still wanted her in his arms, which meant maybe he'd forgive her. She fitted her body against his. The cottage had warmed from the fire, and she'd adapted to the smell of burning guano, so it no longer stung her eyes.

"Cathbad joined me in trance. I didn't call him, he was just there. He said to let the dragons take care of their own problems."

"Likely a wise course of action," she murmured, waiting. Angus would tell her more when he was ready.

He cupped her chin in his hand and tilted her head so she had to look at him. "There's no more to relay about the dragons. According to my kinsman, once I'm done raising our son, I'll be free of the Celts. I have no idea how that will happen."

"What of us?" Despite her resolve to remain quiet, the words found their way out anyway.

"Cathbad didn't know, which could be a good thing. We'll remain apart while I raise our boy, unless you find a way to square your role in the Pantheon with being mother to a child conceived by normal means."

"Did Cathbad cast any light on if I discovered how to do that?"

Angus shook his head. "Nay, but what could be so difficult about—?"

"Doona say it." She pressed an open hand across his mouth. "I doona know if I could escape my role, no matter how much I wanted to. 'Twas assigned by Danu, for reasons only she knows."

Her plea must've gotten through because his muscles, which had felt like granite, relaxed where his body pressed against hers. His words clinched her impression when he said, "I spoke out of turn about something I don't understand. Once our boy is grown," his voice crackled with emotion, "I hope more than anything a way will open for us to find one another again."

She sagged against him relieved to have a path set before them, but heartsick too. How could she live without him? "It could be worse," she said, struggling to not clutch him to her and say to hell with everything.

He brushed his lips over hers. "Aye," he copied her brogue. "It could always be worse. Do you have a place in mind to wait out the pregnancy and nursing?"

She shook her head, interest kindling at his words. "Ye have a reason for asking."

"That I do. I have an idea that might play out well and allow us to see each other from time to time."

"Tell me." The firelight was dying, so she dialed up the lumens in her mage light. It floated to her side like a dutiful servant.

"It might be better to show you. We could do it in this time, but I'd feel better if we took a shot at returning to our own."

Arianrhod glanced at the hearth. Now that the flames weren't powered by magic, they were dying, leaving a bed of glowing coals. She and Angus could leave without worrying about the countryside catching fire. She untangled herself from him and stood. Her bow and quiver were where she'd left them, leaned against the far wall. By the time she'd slung both over her shoulder, he was on his feet, dressed, and ready to leave.

They stepped over the high lintel into a night flooded by moonlight. For once the thick clouds that usually blanketed the U.K. weren't in evidence. She linked her arm through his, and they picked their way down the steep hillside to flatter ground where the time tunnel had forced them out. A flurry of *baahs* was followed by a herd of fluffy sheep, nipping grass as they sashayed past.

"Someone needs to shear them," Angus noted.

"This strain isna known for their wool."

Angus snorted. "I never could tell one type from another. Except Merinos and they're not native to the U.K."

"Och, mayhap ye could start a small sheep ranch. 'Twould give our boy something to do."

"Ari." He came to a halt, forcing her to stop alongside him. "We're on the edge of the twenty-first century. He'll be in school and locked to his mobile phone and computer the rest of the time. That technology is in its infancy right now, but it's growing fast."

"Ye think?" She rolled her eyes. "Betwixt ye and me, he'll have magic to burn." She narrowed her eyes, thinking. "I have the easier job, since he'll still be a biddable toddler when I give him over to you. I doona envy you. He'll not be easy to raise."

A soft light kindled deep in his eyes. "Whatever he is, he'll be ours, and I'll love him and do the best I can by him. Even if it means telling Arawn and them no a time or two."

"What will ye tell them about the boy? They'll not believe a child simply dropped out of the sky and into your lap, and we doona want them looking closely enough to figure out 'tis mine as well."

"If my plan works, that will sort itself out. Shall we try to return to our own time?"

"Let me summon the shaft. Mayhap 'twill be more kindly disposed if I call it."

Her words weren't exactly prophetic. The time tunnel didn't jump to her command for a good half hour, and then it was sluggish to open once it became visible. Arianrhod swallowed irritation, stowing it well beneath the surface. The living entity that infused the time shaft with its power was extraordinarily sensitive to negative emotions.

"Mayhap if I chant 'Om' a time or two, 'twill be happier," she murmured.

"That's the idea." He took her elbow and guided her through the portal. "Radiate peace, tranquility, and a can do attitude."

She laughed, and the walls took on a delighted glow before the doorway shrank into nothingness, and they began to move.

"What's so funny?" He still held onto her arm.

"Hearing modern speech—from any of us. We'll need to pay attention to the nodes since we're not going far. Won't take but a few minutes."

She focused on the nodes, which counted off twenty year bites.

Time travel was far from exact, but she'd gotten better at extrapolating the spaces between nodes. She timed the incantation to release them from the shaft, and it thudded to a halt before an opening formed.

"Not the most elegant transition," she said, "but we're here."

He followed her into the gray light of dawn and inhaled deeply. The metallic scents of modern life and pollution reinforced that they'd come out in the right place. "Thank you for sweet-talking the mechanism into accepting us. If it had just been me, I suspect I'd have had a harder time."

She swung to face him. "Show me what you have in mind. Quickly, afore anyone figures out we've returned."

He nodded and wove a hand around her waist. After a short time, she concluded they were headed for the sea off the tip of Northern Ireland. Something he'd said rattled about in her mind and she asked, "Does this involve the Selkies?"

He cast an approving smile her way. "Aye. You're a canny one."

"Not so much. Ye mentioned them to me, and we're about to walk right into the sea."

"Have you ever spent time with them?" She shook her head, and he continued. "They're an ancient race with memories that stretch in all directions. We could've found them in the last time period where we were, and they would've remembered me, but I thought it best to approach the pod from the time where we'll be living."

Arianrhod closed her teeth over her lower lip, thinking. "Won't the Selkie who sings to you when you make love with her be jealous?"

"Nay. They don't see things like that. They form couples, trios, quads, and more. Their couplings are fluid, and children are raised by the community. Not that they have many, which is why they'll welcome our son."

She stopped walking, absorbing the idea, running its ramifications through her mind. "Ye're suggesting I live with the Selkies until our son is weaned."

He smiled, and his teeth shone very white against his wind-burned skin. "Aye. It would make it possible for me to visit you, and it would also give me a credible explanation for how our boy came to be. Selkies occasionally give birth to half-human children."

"I like it. It could work."

"So long as the Celts don't look too closely." He took a measured breath. "You can think about this next part, but if you remain determined to hide your role in this from your kin, we'll have to alter our child's memories so they're vague where you're concerned."

Outrage laced with maternal protectiveness surged, but she shoved it aside. How could she chide him for speaking the truth? She forced a careful neutrality into her next words. "We doona have to make that choice just yet."

"Nay, we don't. Let's see what the Selkies think and if they'll help." Angus's eyes glittered like exotic gemstones. "At least I'd be able to see you until I have the boy to care for full time."

"Jonathan," she said.

"Huh?" He cocked his head to one side.

"That will be our son's name. We need something to call him, and the name feels right to me."

Angus glanced down for long moments. When he raised his gaze to hers, he cradled the side of her head in a long-fingered hand. "Jonathan it is. Shall we find the Selkies?"

"Aye. Do we call them?"

"We could, but it'd be better if we joined them." He began stripping off clothes, piling rocks atop them in case a brisk wind blew out of nowhere.

She did the same. When they were both naked, they joined hands and walked into the chill, salt surf of the Irish Sea. Once water reached their chests, they stroked for deep water. Angus raised his voice in song to call the Selkies. She couldn't tell where they came from, but the water churned with their warmth and multi-hued pelts.

"Goddess!" rang around her, followed by, *"You honor us with your presence."*

Arianrhod preened. Humans had long since ceased to worship pagan gods. To find that the sea people hadn't forgotten her warmed her spirit and renewed her faith in the future, a future where a child of hers would play a key role.

She followed Angus and the pod deep into the ocean, instructing her lungs to process oxygen from seawater. By the time she was done marveling that she could breathe underwater, they'd closed much of the distance to a structure right out of *The Little Mermaid.* Coral towers in pastel hues rose in a pattern suggestive of a castle. Glowing fish graced its corners, and some variety of numinous kelp hung from what looked like parapets.

The largest seal-creature she'd ever seen emerged from between two stone towers and swam straight toward them. The black Selkie bowed to her and said, *"I am Aegir. Welcome, goddess."*

Before she could reply, he gestured for them to follow him and swam deeper still. Arianrhod stroked through the clear water, swimming by Angus's side, and recalled what she knew about Selkies but didn't come up with much. There had to be more to them than their ability to take human form while carefully hiding their skins, so they wouldn't be trapped on land.

Twisted coral stalks rose around them, and they swam through an underwater forest in whites, pinks, and lavendars. Reminiscent of a maze, the coral reminded her of the Minotaur's lair in Knossos, except far more beautiful.

The coral opened onto a grand hall. Selkies swam in small groups but formed rows once Aegir clapped his flippers together and nodded at Angus. *"Your visit honors us. What can we do for you?"*

"Thank you for the hospitality of your welcome." Angus's words held a formal edge. *"We seek a boon, and there is no time to waste."*

The Selkies turned to gaze at her and Angus. Arianrhod opened her mouth, then laughed. Bubbles rose above her head. Even if she could force her voice out, no one would hear it. She glanced at the fifty or so Selkies. Most were dark brown or black, but a few lighter pelts were in evidence.

"I come to ask a favor of the sea people." She kept the same formalityAngus had adopted. *"I am pregnant with Angus's son. 'Tis a forbidden thing, and the Pantheon would exile me. I seek shelter among you until I have my child and he is weaned."*

"What happens to the child after that?" Aegir asked. He leaned forward, his whiskers quivering with concern.

Another coal black Selkie swam to Angus's side and draped a flipper over him. *"I could raise him after the goddess must return to her world."*

"We all would." Voices rose around her, and it took all Arianrhod's self-control not to cry.

"I will take him once he's weaned," Angus said. *"I saw his future, or the first part of it anyway, in a dream. He is mine to raise."*

"So long as the child will be cared for, we willingly accept our role." Aegir swam to Arianrhod and touched her face with his snout.

The black Selkie next to Angus swam to her side as well. *"I am Celene. I care about Angus too, and I'll help any way I can. Will you be with us from now until the child is weaned?"*

Arianrhod considered Celene's question. The safest path would be for her to stay with the Selkies until it was time to give her child to Angus, but she'd never liked unfinished business.

"I'll be with you soon. First I must visit the Celtic Council and close off some loose ends."

"Are you certain?" Angus asked.

"Aye, quite certain. It willna do anyone any good if the Morrigan turns the world inside out hunting us. And she will. I need to come up with a credible reason why I'll be gone for a while."

"What will that be?" Aegir asked. *"In case one of us is confronted by a Celt. It isn't likely, but it's best to be prepared."*

Arianrhod thought about it. When an answer came, she was pleased by its simplicity. *"I will tell them I must return to Caer Sidi to hone my moon mother magic. Caer Sidi is my special place. 'Tis closed to them, so no one will come looking for me."*

Angus reached for her hand and closed his fingers around hers.

"Find me as soon as you return," Celene said. *"I'll see you're well settled."* She clapped her flippers together, and her jaws spread into a wide smile. *"A child. I'm so excited. I never had pups of my own."*

"Thank you." Angus bowed, awkward in the water.

"Thank you." Aegir bowed back. *"Your faith in us honors the bond you have with our people."*

"I too offer my heartfelt thanks." Arianrhod dipped her head until her hair floated around her, and she skimmed it away from her face.

Angus released her hand. He turned and led the way back through the coral forest. The Selkie pod followed for a while, but by the time Arianrhod's head broke the surface a few yards from shore, they'd vanished. She dragged herself from the surf and directed a stream of magic to dry herself.

"Now for the hard part," she muttered. "For both of us."

"Why for me?" Angus paused from shaking water out of his hair.

"Ye've been grinning like a guilty schoolchild ever since ye found out about Jonathan. I can wipe him from your mind for long enough for ye to check in with Arawn and my brother."

Angus shook his head. "Nay. I'll call my own power to bear on the problem. I plan to move to Ireland, though, to raise our son. Inishowen is closer to the roots of my power, and the land will make it easier for me to keep our secret safe from your kin."

He came toward her, still naked and smelling of the sea when he gathered her into his arms. Joy mingled with newfound power spilled from him in sheaves, and she nestled into his embrace.

"We'll make this work." Her words were muffled against his neck.

"Aye, lass, that we will." He cradled her head in a hand and shifted it so he could see her face. "Another vow I'll make before you and the gods is this. I'll find a way for us to be together. If not in this time and place, then I'll hunt until one shows up. I'll not live out my life without you."

The tears that had been close to the surface in the Selkie's palace trickled from her eyes. She blinked them back. No one had ever forced their way far enough past her prickly exterior to love her—until now. "No matter what happens"—she straightened in his arms—"we'll raise a fine man between us."

"Jonathan aside, don't you want us to be together?" Tension spiked outward in fine lines around his eyes and creases in his forehead.

"Of course I do." She looked away from his direct gaze. "I'm just not as certain as you about finding a place somewhere that will accept us."

He gripped her chin, forcing her to look at him again. "You have to believe, *mo croi,* my heart, my love. You're immortal, and I'll live a long time. Say we'll find a way. Say it, and you'll begin to believe it."

"Can it be so simple?"

"Aye, if you'll let it."

She tossed caution, her ever-present sidekick, to the four winds. "I want to believe you." She stroked the side of his face. "For now, I believe in us and what we've created. Let's take this one step at a time."

"It's a start." He tightened his hold on her back and threaded his other arm around her just before he slashed his mouth down on hers.

She kissed him back, showing him the bone deep longing she didn't have words for in the touch of her flesh against his. At least she wouldn't be totally separated from him. For the next two or three years, he could swim with the Selkies and find her in the sea.

CHAPTER 16

*A*ngus made his way back to Inverness in the Scottish Highlands by himself, via ferryboat and the train. Though he knew how to drive, he'd never thought it worthwhile to own a car. He and Arianrhod had talked about traveling together but decided it was too dangerous.The emotions cascading from them were too fresh to hide if they ran into anyone—a strong possibility since the Celts would be awaiting their return.

Deep in thought and missing her already, he trudged up the steps of a seventeenth century manor housethat had been split into apartments, heading for his on the top floor. Midway he sensed angry Celts and stopped to compose himself. That done, he prodded with a tendril of magic and frowned. Maybe the Celts weren't exactly angry, but neither were they waiting to congratulate him on carrying out their orders.

With a small prayer to Cathbad to help him appear nothing more than a weary traveler finally home from a difficult assignment, he wound layers of illusion around himself as he tackled the last three flights of stairs. He manufactured a stunned expression before loosing a jot of magic to twist the deadbolt on his door—and widened his eyes still farther as he stepped through.

"Och! What a surprise." Angus stopped just inside the lintel. His lodging was one large room that served as both living- and bedrooms, with a small kitchen off to one side. The bathroom was down the hall. He'd never taken time to decorate, so the walls were bare, but books and scrolls littered every surface and sat in piles on the floor. A computer and monochrome monitor sprawled across a generous table pushed into one corner. He'd never wanted them, but the technology wouldn't go away, so he was forcing himself to learn about it.

"Finally!" Arawn, god of the dead, lounged in the room's only comfortable chair, his long legs splayed before him. Dark hair spilled down his chest. For once it was unbound, rather than done up in the Celtic braiding pattern he favored. Buff-colored battle leathers hugged his lean form, and shrewd dark eyes homed in on Angus.

"Finally, what?" Angus shucked his small travel pack and dropped it on the floor before perching on the edge of his bed. "Am I late for something?"

"That depends." Gwydion, master enchanter and Arianrhod's brother, stepped out of the small kitchen cradling a mug of something that smelled like coffee between his hands. His blond hair was braided in many small rows, close against his head, and his blue eyes held a guarded edge. He wore his usual magician's robes, cream-colored this time and sashed in red. A leather belt studded with pouches of herbs and other accoutrements hung low about his hips. When Angus glanced around for the warrior magician's ever-present staff, he noticed the intricately carved wooden rod leaning against a wall.

The irritation he usually went to great lengths to mask rolled from him in waves. Good, maybe it would cover other things. "What the hell?" He curled one hand into a fist and pounded it against his thigh. "I did what you sent me to, and damn near got myself killed in the process—"

"Aye, but what did ye do to piss off the Morrigan?" Arawn broke in. He cocked his head to one side, still staring intently at Angus.

"Refused to fuck her."

"We figured it was something like that." Gwydion sent a knowing glance skittering across the room at Arawn. "Start at the beginning. How'd ye end up in the Morrigan's clutches anyway?"

"And in Rhukon's time to boot," Arawn added.

Angus answered their questions with one of his own. "Is the Morrigan complaining about me?"

"Aye, ye doona know the half of it, laddie." Arawn barked out a short laugh. "She's demanding the Council remand you to her for an indefinite time."

Angus grimaced, remembering the slimy feel of the Battle Crow's energy, no matter what form she took. "Surely you told her nay." He glanced from Arawn to Gwydion, but neither Celt said anything. "If you didn't refuse, what did you say?"

"That we'd find you and figure out what comes next." Arawn grinned.

"If ye mucked up this last assignment, we may let her have her head with you for a bit." Gwydion smirked.

"The hell. That'll never happen." Angus shot to his feet and stalked across the room until he was nose to nose with the Celt. "Give me that." He grabbed Gwydion's mug, took a long drink, and swiped his hand across the back of his mouth before handing it back.

"Gotten gutsy." Gwydion quirked a white-blond brow. "Ye may as well take the coffee. I can brew more. Sit and tell us what happened. Ye have a different feel about you."

"Aye, 'tis more than just the dragon shifter problem," Arawn concurred. He skewered Angus with his dark gaze, probing his mind, but Angus held him at bay easily, pleased by the small victory.

He snatched the mug back and made his way to a straight-backed chair beneath a window, his mind churning furiously. He'd have to tell them something credible. By the time he settled and crossed his legs, he'd figured it out.

"Rhukon didn't give me the answers I needed, so I cast a trance state. Cathbad found me." Angus pushed slender threads of magic behind his words to assess their impact.

Arawn shrugged. "'Twas bound to happen sooner or later."

Relief surged, but Angus batted it down. He'd fed them a small piece of truth, and they weren't going to dig deeper. At least he hoped they wouldn't. He paid out a little more information. "Once he found me, I followed him backward in time, but didn't remain long."

"The more salient question is what ye're going to do, now ye know."Gwydion nailed him with his sharp-eyed gaze.

"Nothing."

"'Tis hard to believe," Arawn said. "After all your fussing about knowing your origins."

"I've been forbidden from returning to my own time. It turns out I have something to do here."

"What exactly might that be?" Gwydion inquired archly.

Angus shrugged. "I have no idea. Cathbad didn't say."

"Just so ye're clear your orders come from us, not him," Arawn said with flared nostrils and a stern, chilly voice.

Angus wanted to punch him. Anything to knock the supercilious expression off his face.

Angus set the coffee on the windowsill and straightened in his chair until he faced Arawn squarely. "I won't always be your errand boy, your lackey. Exactly how things go from here will depend on the level of respect I get."

Gwydion narrowed his eyes. "The lad has a point. This is a game-changer, and we'd be wise to recognize it."

Before Arawn could argue the point, Angus broke in. "Do you want to hear what happened on this last assignment or not? If not, I'd appreciate space to grab an hour's sleep."

"Ye're jumping on this equality thing with both feet," Arawn observed dryly.

"Give it a rest," Gwydion snapped at his fellow god before turning to Angus. "Aye, we want to hear. The Morrigan's waiting, among other things."

"First off, you don't have the right to offer me to anyone." Angus looked from one Celt to the other from under hooded lids. "Second, I'll fight you to the death before I spend any more time in her presence."

"We werena serious about that." Arawn gestured with one hand. "Start at the beginning and tell us everything that happened."

Surprise took root and spread deep within Angus, but he took care to shield it. That Arawn backed off his threat about the Morrigan so easily might bode well. He tilted his chair until it rested against the wall and started talking.

"I met the dragon Eletea near the Irish Sea off Inishowen as you instructed…"

The story took longer than he imagined it would, since one or the other Celt interrupted constantly. They were particularly curious about his time with Cathbad. Neither asked anything about Arianrhod, which seemed like it might be a good thing.

Angus laced his fingers together. "After the time shaft allowed us back inside, it returned us to Inishowen. I spent a spot of time with a Selkie I'm fond of and returned here."

"A Selkie is it?" Interest flickered in Arawn's eyes.

Gwydion, who'd never sat, crooked a finger at Arawn. "He can tell us about his new friend later. Best be on our way afore the Morrigan hunts us down."

"Agreed." Arawn flowed to his feet, lithe and graceful. "Ye may rest." He directed his words at Angus. "Once ye're refreshed, I expect you to join us at the council chambers in Inverlochy Castle."

Angus stood too. "Will the Morrigan be there?"

"Like as not." Arawn met his gaze evenly. "As ye've pointed out, we canna foist you off onto her, no matter what she wants."

"Thank the gods." Angus blew out a noisy breath. "That old hag gives me the creeps."

"Sometimes she can appear quite attractive." Gwydion winked lewdly.

"Doesn't matter what she looks like," Angus replied. "She still has a putrid smell and a hungry desperation that makes me want to run the other way—or bash her skull in."

Arawn tossed his head back and laughed. When he got himself under control, he said, "I doona suggest the latter. She loves conflict, and she'll clean your clock."

Angus wasn't so certain about that, but he kept his mouth shut, waiting until the Celts were well and truly gone before cautiously letting the layers of magic he'd shielded himself with slip away. He bent to unlace his boots and toed them off before making himself comfortable on his narrow bed. He still slept on the same mattress he'd had for years, not seeing any reason to change it for something larger.

When he closed his eyes, an image of Arianrhod shimmered before him. Lost in a vision of her silvery hair and gold and silver eyes, he let sleep take him.

ARIANRHOD TRAMPED up the steps of the ruins of Inverlochy Castle, wanting to get the next hour or two over with. She'd done what she could to drive her private thoughts to an even deeper place than usual, and she hoped she appeared her old, imperious self when she strode along vast hallways and through the twelve-foot tall carved wooden doors leading to the council chambers.

Heads snapped up at her arrival, and Arianrhod trotted briskly into the familiar chamber decorated with crystals and natural stone in every hue of the rainbow. Thick carpets covered scarred wooden floors; ever-changing scenes from Celtic battles marched across them, fueled by magic. A fire burned in the enormous hearth that took up one end of the room, and Ceridwen sat before it stirring her cauldron as usual. The goddess of the world got to her feet, but before she could say anything, the Morrigan—in crow form—planted herself firmly in front of Arianrhod.

"Ye decided to return, eh?" The crow cackled nastily. "Took your sweet time about it."

Arianrhod rolled her eyes. "Ye're just out of sorts because Angus dinna wish to fuck you."

"I've taken care of that little problem. Arawn and your brother will deliver him to me soon." She clacked her beak shut twice for emphasis.

Arianrhod gnashed her teeth together and made shooing motions with both hands. "Get out of my way. I could care less about your love life."

"Not how it was looking to me." The Morrigan latched her beady, avian eyes onto Arianrhod, who snarled at her.

"Stand down. Both of you," Ceridwen thundered. She drove her stirring rod against the wooden floorboards at her feet for emphasis, and lightning forked from its tip.

The Battle Crow squawked and flapped her enormous wings before moving aside just enough for Arianrhod to sweep past her. "I'm not done." The crow snapped her beak microns from Arianrhod's ear.

She halted and turned to face the Morrigan. "Aye, but ye are. I'm sick to death of you and your posturing. Leave me be."

"Ye canna talk thus to me." The crow flew at her, and Arianrhod spiraled a funnel of magic to block her.

Andraste, goddess of victory, surged to her feet, long blonde curls flying about her. "Oberon's balls! A battle. Things were growing a bit dull." She pumped both fists in the air, her green eyes snapping in anticipation.

"Not here there won't be." Ceridwen slammed her staff on the floor again. Light shot from both it and the cauldron this time. She stomped up the center of the room and grabbed one of the Morrigan's wingtips. "Ye behave, or ye leave."

"I canna leave. I'm waiting for Arawn to deliver Angus to me." The crow tossed her head.

"If he wanted aught to do with you, he'd have taken you on Rhukon's moorlands." Arianrhod bit off the words. "Ye make his skin crawl. He told me so."

"Shut up!" the crow screeched. "Bitch! Slut!"

"Och aye, 'tis getting better and better." Andraste strode closer, presumably for a clearer view.

Arianrhod figured the Morrigan would've taken another run at her, but Ceridwen stood between them. "Behave or leave," she repeated and twisted the Morrigan's wing until black feathers fluttered to the floor. "If I'm forced to tell you a third time, I'll banish you from these chambers for a hundred years." Determination and danger flashed from her dark eyes, and she shoved dark hair shot with silver behind her shoulders.

The air around the crow took on insubstantial edges. Moments later, the Morrigan was gone. Breath whistled through Arianrhod's clenched teeth. "Ye shouldna have done that," she told Ceridwen.

"Whyever not?" The goddess of the world eyed her coolly.

"Because she's knee-deep in whatever poison has infiltrated the dragon shifter bond, and now we canna question her."

"We could call her back." Still on her feet, Andraste sounded hopeful.

"We will if we have to." Ceridwen screwed her face into a distasteful grimace. "No matter what hellish plot the Morrigan is mixed up in this time, the air in these chambers is much easier to breathe without her here."

Ceridwen crooked a finger at Arianrhod before she turned and started for her cauldron at the far end of the room.

"Och. Fun's over. Too bad." Andraste made her way back to a pile of battle armor she'd been rubbing rust spots from. No one used it anymore, but the goddess of victory made occasional trips to the past decked out like a Valkyrie. Arianrhod had accompanied her a time or two.

Noticing the direction of her gaze, Andraste waved cheerily. Arianrhod smiled before she trotted after Ceridwen, breathing a little easier. The Morrigan made the first part effortless. Now all she had to do was get through a recitation of what occurred with the dragons, dragon shifters, and Rhukon, and she'd be done here—at least for a few years.

Ceridwen twisted to face her and spun earth power around them, so no one could eavesdrop on their conversation. The air took on a silvery hue. "Tell me," she said without preamble. "Everything."

Arianrhod talked so long her throat grew dry, but she didn't want to break the magic surrounding them to pour herself some wine. "...And so, there's at least one more corrupt mage seeking to bond with a dragon. Rhukon and Connor are still at large. For all I know, there may be others, but the dragons are deep into figuring things out."

"What of Lachlan and Britta and their dragons? I held concern about them afore I sent you to Fire Mountain."

"Like I said, Rhukon—and the Morrigan—likely know exactly where they are."

Ceridwen tilted her chin at a bold angle. "That will be your next assignment."

Arianrhod shook her head. "Nay. I doona work for you."

The goddess of the world drew her dark brows together across her high forehead until they formed an unbroken line. "Ye'd defy me?"

At the fury flaring from Ceridwen's eyes, Arianrhod tossed words into the fray. "Doona characterize it as defiance. I told you I spent time with Cathbad—twice. I met with him in his own time, and he came to me in a vision. My path for the next span of time is to sequester myself in Caer Sidi. I must hone my moon mother skills to ensure the tides remain constant. Men have mucked up the environment so thoroughly, neither are holding a consistent pattern."

"I could accompany you. Hurry things along." Ceridwen shot a disingenuous smile her way.

"I'd love to have your help, but ye canna enter Caer Sidi. 'Tis my magical realm, and mine alone."

Ceridwen frowned. "Och, and I'd forgotten that."

Like hell ye did.

"If 'tis all the same to you, I'll take my leave." Arianrhod ginned up a smile. "If the dragon shifters are still a problem when I return, I'll pick up the banner then."

Ceridwen's spell crashed about them. It made such an unholy racket Arianrhod started, but she recognized dismissal and hurried across the breadth of the huge, circular room.

Almost. I'm nearly out of here.

Before she made the doors, they swung open, and Arawn and Gwydion marched through. "Sister!" Gwydion bowed low.

She rolled her eyes. "Welcome to you too. I was just on my way out."

"Obviously. To where?" Arawn's dark gaze held what looked like more than mild curiosity.

She squared her shoulders. "'Tis my time to enter contemplation in Caer Sidi. The moon and tides require my full attention."

"Not so fast." Gwydion latched a hand around her upper arm. "What exactly did ye have to do with Cathbad finding Angus?"

"I resent that." Arianrhod glared at him. "Cathbad found his kinsman easily enough when we were closer to his own time. I merely came along for the ride."

Gwydion examined her through slitted eyes. "Aye, but there's more to that story."

"Nay, there's not. Let go of me." She wrenched her arm from his grasp.

"Humph." Arawn swept the room with discerning eyes. "Where's the Morrigan?"

"She left." Arianrhod spat the words out.

"Just as well," Gwydion muttered. "I wasna looking forward to telling her Angus dinna wish her company."

Ceridwen made her way to where they stood. "Hello, men," she purred. "Welcome."

"Och, whenever she sounds like that, she wants something." Gwydion made a face that looked like he'd bitten into something rotten.

"Now that ye mention it," Ceridwen continued, her voice silky sweet, "we must craft a plan to locate the missing dragon shifters—"

"I'll leave you to it then." Arianrhod bolted for the door before anyone could react and call her back. Relief ran deep once she exited Inverlochy's ruins, and the damp air of the Scottish Highlands enveloped her.

In case anyone chose to track her energy, she summoned a spell to split the worlds and take her to Caer Sidi. She'd remain long enough to make certain everything in her realm remained untouched before heading for the Selkie pod swimming in the Irish Sea. Angus would be there. She felt certain of it, and she wasn't ready to give him up.

Not quite yet.

You've reached the end of *Highland Secrets*. I'd sure appreciate it if you'd leave a review.

This series continues in *To Love a Highland Dragon*, Dragon Lore, Book Two. Read on for a sample.

ABOUT THE AUTHOR

Ann Gimpel is a USA Today bestselling author. She's also a clinical psychologist, with a Jungian bent, and a vagabond at heart. Avocations include mountaineering, skiing, wilderness photography and, of course, writing. A lifelong aficionado of the unusual, she began writing speculative fiction a few years ago. Since then her short fiction has appeared in a number of webzines and anthologies. Her longer books run the gamut from urban fantasy to paranormal romance. She's published over 70 books to date, with several more planned for 2019 and beyond. A husband, grown children, grandchildren and three wolf hybrids round out her family.

Keep up with her at www.anngimpel.com or http://anngimpel.blogspot.com

If you enjoyed what you read, get in line for special offers and pre-release special reads. Sign up for Ann's newsletter on her website or her blog.

TO LOVE A HIGHLAND DRAGON

DRAGON LORE BOOK TWO

Kheladin listened to the rush of blood as his multi-chambered heart pumped. After eons of nothingness, the unexpected sound surprised him. A cool, sandy floor pressed against his scaled haunches. One whirling eye flickered open, followed by the other.

Where am I?

He peered at his surroundings and blew out a sigh, followed by steam, smoke, and fire.

Thanks be to Dewi—Kheladin invoked the blood-red Celtic dragon goddess—*I'm still in my cave. It smelled right, but I wasna certain.*

He rotated his serpent's head atop his long, sinuous neck. Vertebrae cracked. Kheladin lowered his head and scanned the place he and Lachlan, his human bondmate, had barricaded themselves into. It might've only been days ago, but somehow, it didn't seem like days, or even months or a few years. His body felt rusty, as if he hadn't used it in centuries.

How long did I sleep?

He shook his head. Copper scales flew everywhere, clanking against a pile littered around him. More than anything, the glittery

181

heap reinforced his belief he'd been asleep for a very long time. Dragons shed their scales annually. From the amount circling his body, he'd gone through hundreds of molt cycles. But how? The last thing he remembered was retreating to his cave far beneath Lachlan's castle and working with the mage to construct strong wards.

Had the black wyvern grown powerful enough to force his magic into the very heart of Kheladin's fortress?

If that's true—if we really were his prisoner, why'd I finally waken? Is Lachlan still within me?

Stop! I have to take things one at a time.

He returned his gaze to the nooks and crannies of his spacious cave. He'd have to take inventory, but it appeared his treasure hadn't been disturbed. Kheladin blew a plume of steam upward, followed by an experimental gout of fire. The black wyvern, his sworn enemy since before the Crusades, may have bested him, but he hadn't gotten his slimy talons on any of Kheladin's gold or jewels.

He shook out his back feet and shuffled to the pool at one end of the cave where he dipped his snout and drank deeply. The water didn't taste quite right. It wasn't poisoned, but it held an undercurrent of metals that had never been there before. Kheladin rolled the liquid around in his mouth. He didn't recognize much of what he tasted, but he was thirsty and it seemed safe enough, so he drank some more.

The flavors aren't familiar because I've been asleep for so long. Aye, that must be it. Part of his mind recoiled; he suspected he was deluding himself.

"*We're awake.*" Lachlan's voice hummed in the dragon's mind.

"*Aye, that we are.*"

"*How long did we sleep?*"

"*I doona know.*" Water streamed down the dragon's snout and neck. He knew what would come next, and he didn't have to wait long.

"Let's shift. We think better in my body." Lachlan urged Kheladin to cede ascendency.

"I doona agree." Kheladin pushed back. *"I was figuring things out afore ye woke."*

"Aye, I'm certain ye were, but..." But what? *"Och aye, my brain is thick and fuzzy, as if I havena used it for a verra long time."*

"Mine feels the same."

The bond allowed only one form at a time. Since they were in Kheladin's body, he had the upper hand. Lachlan wasn't strong enough to force a shift without his help. There'd been a time when he could have but not now.

Was it safe to venture above ground?

Kheladin recalled the last day he'd seen the sun. After a vicious battle in the great room of Lachlan's castle, they'd retreated to his cave and taken their dragon form as a final resort. Rhukon, the black wyvern, pretended he wanted peace. He'd come with an envoy that turned out to be a retinue of heavily armed men.

Both he and Lachlan expected Rhukon to follow them underground. Kheladin's last thought, before nothingness descended, was disbelief because their enemy hadn't pursued them.

Humph. He did *come after us but with magic. Magic strong enough to penetrate our wards.*

"Aye, and I was thinking the same thing," Lachlan sniped in a vexed tone.

"We trusted him," Kheladin snarled. *"More the fools we were. We should've known."* Despite drinking, his throat was still raw. He sucked more water down and fought rising anger at himself for being gullible. Even if Lachlan hadn't known better, he should've. His stomach cramped from hunger.

Kheladin debated the wisdom of making his way through the warren of tunnels leading to the surface in dragon form. There were always far more humans than dragons. Mayhap it would be wiser to accede to Lachlan's wishes before they crept from their underground lair to rejoin the world of men.

"Grand idea." Lachlan's response was instantaneous, as was his first stab at shifting.

It took half a dozen attempts. Kheladin was far weaker than he imagined and Lachlan so feeble he was almost an impediment. Finally, once a shower of scales cleared, Lachlan's emaciated body stood barefoot and naked in the cave.

LACKING the sharp night vision he enjoyed as a dragon, because his magic was so diminished, Lachlan kindled a mage light and glanced down at himself. Ribs pressed against his flesh, and a full beard extended halfway down his chest. Turning his head to both sides, he saw shoulder blades so sharp he was surprised they didn't puncture his skin. Tawny hair fell in tangles past his waist. The only thing he couldn't see was his eyes. Absent a glass, he was certain they were the same crystal-clear emerald color they'd always been.

He stumbled across the cave to a chest where he kept clothing. Dragons didn't need such silly accoutrements; humans did. He sucked in a harsh breath. The wooden chest was falling to ruin. He tilted the lid against a wall, but it canted to one side. Many of his clothes had moldered into unusable rags, but items toward the bottom fared better. He found a cream-colored linen shirt with long, flowing sleeves, a black and green plaid embroidered with the insignia of his house—a dragon in flight—and soft, deerskin boots that laced to his knees.

He slid the shirt over his head and wrapped the plaid around himself, taking care to wind the tartan so its telltale insignia was hidden in its folds. Who knew if the black wyvern—or his agents— lurked near the mouth of the cave? Lachlan bent to lace his boots. A crimson cloak with only a few moth holes completed his outfit. He finger-combed his hair and smoothed his unruly beard.

"Good God, but I must look a fright," he muttered. "Mayhap I can sneak into the castle and set things aright afore anyone sees me.

Surely my kinsmen will be glad the master of the house has finally returned."

Lachlan worked on bolstering a confidence he was far from feeling. He'd nearly made it to the end of the cave, where a rock-strewn path led upward, when he doubled back to get a sword and scabbard—just in case things weren't as sanguine as he hoped. He located a thigh sheath and a short dagger as well, fumbling to attach them beneath his kilt. Underway once again, he hadn't made it very far along the upward-sloping tunnel that ended at a well-hidden opening not far from the postern gate of his castle, when he ran into rocks littering the way.

He worked his way around progressively larger boulders until he came to a huge one that totally blocked the passageway. Lachlan stared at it in disbelief. When had that happened? In all the time he'd been using these paths, they'd never been blocked by rock fall. If he weren't so weak, summoning magic to shove the rock over enough to allow him to pass wouldn't be a problem. As it was, simply walking uphill proved a challenge.

He pinched the bridge of his nose between a grimy thumb and forefinger. His mage light weakened.

If I can't even keep a light going, how in the goddess's name will I be able to move that rock?

Lachlan hunkered next to the boulder and let his light die while he ran possibilities through his head. His stomach growled and clenched in hunger. Had he come through however much time had passed to cower like a dog in his own cave?

"No, by God." He slammed a fist against the boulder, and it went right on through. The air sizzled. Magic. The rock was illusion. Not real.

Counter spell. I need a counter spell.

Mayhap I doona.

He stood and took a deep breath before walking into the huge rock. The air did more than sizzle. It flamed. If he'd been human, it would've burned him to ashes, but dragons were impervious to fire, as were dragon shifters. Lachlan waltzed through the rock, cursing Rhukon as he went. Five more boulders blocked his tunnel, each more charged with magic than the last.

Finally, sweating and cursing, he rounded the last curve, and the air ahead grew brighter. He wanted to throw himself on the ground and screech his triumph.

Not a good idea.

"Let me out. Ye have no idea what we'll find."

Kheladin's voice in his mind was welcome but the idea wasn't. *"Ye're right. Because we have no idea what's out there, we stay in my skin until we're certain. We can hide in this form far more easily than we can in yours."*

"Since when did we take to hiding?" The dragon sounded outraged.

"Our magic is weak." Lachlan adopted a placating tone. *"'Tis prudent to be cautious until it fully recovers."*

"No dragon would ever say such a thing." Deep, fiery frustration rolled off Kheladin.

Steam belched from Lachlan's mouth. *"Stop that,"* he hissed, but his mind voice was all but obliterated by wry dragon laughter.

"Why? I find it amusing ye think an eight foot tall dragon with elegant copper scales and handsome, green eyes would be difficult to sequester." Kheladin paused a beat. *"And infuriating we need to conceal ourselves at all. Need I remind you we're warriors?"*

"Of course we're warriors," Lachlan said affably, sidestepping the issue of hiding. He didn't want to risk being goaded into something unwise. Kheladin chuckled and pushed more steam through Lachlan's mouth, punctuated by a few flames.

Lost in a sudden rush of memories, Lachlan slowed his pace. As a mage, he would've lived hundreds of years, but bonded to a dragon, he'd live forever. In preparation, he'd studied long years with Aether, a wizard and dragon shifter himself. Along the way, Lachlan forsook much—a wife and bairns, for starters, for what woman would put up with a husband so rarely at home?—to bond with a dragon, forming their partnership. Once Lachlan's magic was finally strong enough, there'd been the niggling problem of locating that special dragon willing to join its life with his.

Because the bond conferred immortality on both the dragon and their human partner, dragons were notoriously picky. After all, dragon and mage would be welded through eternity. The magic could be undone, but the price was high. Mages were stripped of power, and their dragon mates lost much of theirs too, as the bond unraveled. Rumor suggested that mages who became dragon-less risked madness—an additional stumbling block and strong incentive to choose wisely.

Lachlan hunted for over a hundred years before finding Kheladin. The pairing was instantaneous on both sides. He'd just settled in with his dragon, and was about to chase down a wife to grace his castle, when the black wyvern attacked.

Rhukon had approached Kheladin long before Lachlan, but the dragon rejected the bond, spawning their animosity. That Rhukon finally acquired a dragon of his own hadn't lessened his ill will.

"What are ye waiting for?" Kheladin sounded testy. *"Daydreaming is a worthless pursuit. My grandmother is two thousand years old, and she moves faster than you."*

Lachlan snorted. He didn't bother to explain there wasn't much point in jumping right into Rhukon's arms through the opening in the gorse and thistle bushes growing at the mouth of the cave. An unusual whirring filled the air, like the noisiest beehive he'd ever heard. His heart sped up, but the sound receded.

"What the hell was that?" he muttered and made his way closer to the world outside Kheladin's cave.

Lachlan shoved some overgrown bushes out of the way and peered through. What he saw was so unbelievable, he squeezed his eyes shut tight before opening them and looking again. Unfortunately, nothing had changed. Worse, an ungainly, shiny cylinder roared past, making the same whirring noise he'd puzzled over moments before. He fell backward into the cave, breath harsh in his throat, and landed on his rump.

Lachlan shook his head and balled his hands into fists. Frustration and disbelief battered him, making him wonder if he'd died only to waken in Hell. Not only was the postern gate no longer there, neither was his castle. A long, unattractive row of attached structures stood in its stead.

"Holy godhead. What do we do now?"

"Go out there and hunt down something to eat," the dragon growled.

Lachlan gritted his teeth until his jaw ached. Kheladin had a good point. It was hard to think on an empty stomach.

"Here I was worried about Rhukon. At least I understood him. I fear whatever lies in wait for us will require all our skill."

"Ye were never a coward. 'Tis why I allowed the bond. Get moving."

The dragon's words settled him. Ashamed of his indecisiveness, Lachlan got to his feet. He brushed dirt off his plaid and worked his way through the bushes hiding the cave's entrance. As he untangled stickers from the finely spun wool of his cloak and his plaid, he gawked at a very different world from the one he'd left. There wasn't a field—or an animal—in sight. Roadways paved with something other than dirt and stones were punctuated by structures so numerous, they made him dizzy. The hideous incursion onto his lands stretched in every direction. Lachlan curled his hands into fists again.

He'd find out what happened, by God. When he did, he'd make whoever erected all those abominations take them down.

An occasional person walked by in the distance. They shocked him even more than the buildings and roads. For starters, the males weren't wearing plaids, so there was no way to tell their clan. Females were immodestly covered. Many sported bare legs and breeks so tight he saw the separation between their ass cheeks. Lachlan's groin stirred, his cock hardening. Were the lassies no longer engaging in modesty or subterfuge and simply asking to be fucked? Or was this some new garb that befit a new era?

He detached the last thorn, finally clear of the thicket of sticker bushes. Where could he find a market with vendors? Did market day still exist in this strange environment?

"Holy crap! A kilt, and an old-fashioned one at that. Tad bit early in the day for a costume ball, isn't it?" A rich female voice laced with amusement sounded behind him.

Lachlan spun, hands raised to call magic. He stopped dead once his gaze settled on a lass nearly as tall as himself, which meant she was close to six feet. She turned so she faced him squarely. Bare legs emerged from torn fabric that stopped just south of her female parts. Full breasts strained against scraps of material attached to strings tied around her neck and back. Her feet were encased in a few straps of leather. Long, blonde hair eddied around her, the color of sheaves of summer wheat.

His cock jumped to attention. He itched to make a grab for her breasts or her ass. She had an amazing ass: round and high and tight. What was expected of him? The lass was dressed in such a way as to invite him to simply tear what passed for breeks aside and enter her. Had the world changed so drastically that women provoked men into public sex? He glanced about, half expecting to see couples having it off with one another willy-nilly.

"Well," she urged. "Cat got your tongue?" She placed her hands on her hips. The motion stretched the tiny bits of flowered fabric that barely covered her nipples still further.

Lachlan bowed formally. He straightened and waited for her to hold out a hand for him to kiss. "I'm Lachlan Moncrieffe, my lady. 'Tis a pleasure to—"

She erupted into laughter—and didn't hold out her hand. "I'm Maggie," she managed between gouts of mirth. "What are you? A throwback to medieval times? You can drop the Sir Galahad routine."

Lachlan felt his face heat. "I fear I doona understand the cause of your merriment…my lady."

Maggie rolled midnight blue eyes. "Oh, brother. Did you escape from a mental hospital? Nah, you'd be in pajamas then, not those fancy duds." She dropped her hands to her sides and started to walk past him.

"No. Wait. Please, wait." Lachlan cringed at the whining tone in his voice. The dragon was correct that the Moncrieffe was a proud house. They bowed to no one.

She eyed him askance. "What?"

"I'm a stranger in this town." He winced at the lie. Once upon a time, he'd been master of these lands. Apparently that time had long since passed. "I'm footsore and hungry. Where might I find victuals and ale?"

Her eyes widened. Finely arched blonde brows drew together over a straight nose dotted by a few freckles. "Victuals and ale," she repeated disbelievingly.

"Aye. Food and drink, in the common vernacular."

"Oh, I understood you well enough," Maggie murmured. "Your words, anyway. Your accent's a bit off." His stomach growled again, embarrassingly loud. "Guess you weren't kidding about being hungry." She eyed him appraisingly. "Do you have any money?"

Money. Too late he thought of the piles of gold coins and priceless gems lying on the floor of Kheladin's cave. In the world he'd left, his word was as good as his gold. He opened his mouth, but she waved him to silence. "I'll stand you for a pint and some fish and chips. You can treat me next time."

He heard her mutter, "Yeah right," under her breath as she curled a hand around his arm and tugged. "Come on. I have a couple hours, and then I've got to go to work. I'm due in at three today."

Lachlan trotted along next to her. She let go of him like he was a viper when he tried to close a hand over the one she'd laid so casually on his person. He cleared his throat and wondered what he could safely ask that wouldn't give his secrets away. He could scarcely believe this alien landscape was Scotland, but if he asked what country they were in, or what year it was, she'd think him mad.

Had the black wyvern had used some diabolical dark magic to

transport Kheladin's cave to another locale? Probably not. Even Rhukon wasn't that powerful.

"In here." She pointed to a door beneath a flashing sigil.

He gawked at it. One minute it was red, the next blue, the next green, illuminating the word *Open*. What manner of magic was this?

"Don't tell me you have temporal lobe epilepsy." She stared at him. "It's only a neon sign. It doesn't bite. Move through the door. There's food on the other side," she added slyly.

Feeling like a rube, Lachlan searched for a latch. When he didn't find one, he pushed his shoulder against the door. It opened, and he held it with a hand so Maggie could enter first. "After you, my lady," he murmured.

"Stop that." She spoke into his ear as she went past. "No more *my ladies*. Got it?"

"Aye. Got it." He followed her into a low ceilinged room lined with wooden planks. It was the first thing that looked familiar. Parts of it, anyway. Men—kilt-less men—sat at the bar, hefting glasses and chatting. The tables were empty.

"What'll it be, Mags?" a man with a towel tied around his waist called from behind the bar.

"Couple of pints and two of today's special. Come to think of it..." She eyed Lachlan so intently it made him squirm. "Make that three of the special."

"May I inquire what the special is?" Lachlan asked, thinking he might want to order something different.

Maggie waved a hand at a black board suspended over the bar. "It's right there. If you can't read it—"

"Of course, I can read." He resented the inference he might be uneducated but swallowed back harsh words.

"Excellent. Then move."

She shoved her body into his in a distressingly familiar way for such a communal location. Not that he wouldn't have enjoyed the contact if they were alone, and he were free to take advantage of it.

"All the way to the back," she hissed into his ear. "That way if you slip up, no one will hear."

He bristled. Lachlan Moncrieffe did *not* sit in the back of any establishment. He was always given a choice table near the center of things. He opened his mouth to protest but thought better of it.

She scooped an armful of flattened scrolls off the bar before following him to the back of the room. Once there, she dumped them on the table between them. He wanted to ask what they were but decided he should pretend to know. He turned the top sheaf of papers toward him and scanned the close-spaced print. Many of the words were unfamiliar, but what leapt off the page was *The Inverness Courier* and presumably the current date: June 10, 2012.

His heart thudded in his ears, deafening him with the roar of rushing blood, as he stared at the date.

It had been 1683 when Rhukon chivied him into the dragon's cave. Three hundred twenty-nine years ago, give or take a month or two. At least he was still in Inverness—for all the good it did him.

"You look as if you just saw a ghost." Maggie spoke quietly.

"Nay. I'm quite fine. Thank you for inquiring…my, er…" Lachlan shut up. Anything he said was bound to be wrong.

"Good." She nodded approvingly. "You're learning." The bartender slapped two mugs of ale on the scarred wooden table.

"On your tab, Mags?" he asked.

She nodded. "Except you owe me so much, you'll never catch up."

Still shell-shocked by the realization hundreds of years had slipped past while he and Kheladin slept, Lachlan took a sip of what turned out to be weak ale. It wasn't half bad but could've stood an infusion of bitters. Because it was easier than thinking about his problems, he puzzled over what Maggie meant about the barkeep *owing her so much he'd never catch up.* Why would the barkeep owe her? His nostrils flared. She must work for the establishment— probably as a damsel of ill repute from the looks of her. Mayhap, she hadn't been paid her share of whatever she earned in quite some time.

Protectiveness flared deep inside him. Maggie shouldn't have to earn her way lying on her back. He'd see to it she had a more seemly position.

Aye, once I find my way around this bizarre new world.

Money wouldn't be a problem, but changing three-hundred-year-old gold coins into today's tender might prove challenging. Surely banks existed that could accomplish something like that.

One thing at a time.

"So." She skewered him with her blue gaze—Norse eyes if he'd ever seen a set—and took a sip from her mug. "What did you see in the newspaper that upset you so much?"

"Nothing." He tried for an offhand tone.

"Bullshit," she said succinctly. "I'm a doctor. A psychiatrist. I read people's faces quite well, and you look as if you're perilously close to going into shock."